D0810684

Final Curtain

Philip Ardagh's passion for writing is matched only by his height, his shoe size and the length of his beard. His physical beauty is matched only by the beauty of his prose. He lists his hobbies as 'none of your business' and is a regular face (along with the rest of his body) at book-related events across Britain and Ireland as well as on the Continent and in the US (which is a shorter way of writing USA). He is cheerful in the mornings and kind to animals.

PHILIP ARDAGH

FINAL CURTAIN

Book Three of
The Further Adventures of Eddie Dickens

illustrated by David Roberts

faber and faber

First published in 2006
by Faber and Faber Limited
3 Queen Square, London WC1N 3AU

Typeset by Faber and Faber Limited
Printed in England by Mackays of Chatham plc, Chatham, Kent

Philip Ardagh is hereby identified as author of this work in accordance
with Section 77 of the Copyright, Designs and Patents Act 1988

A CIP record for this book
is available from the British Library

ISBN 978–0-571–21711–3
ISBN 0-571–21711–7

2 4 6 8 10 9 7 5 3 1

In memory of
Stephen Cartwright.
It was fun.

A Message from the Author

Who's invested in a big box of hankies

Well, this is the end of the road as far as Eddie's Further Adventures are concerned. First, there was the original trilogy which began with *Awful End*, and then this one, which started off with Eddie Dickens in the heathery highlands of Scotland in *Dubious Deeds*. Blimey. Six books. Who would have believed it, especially when Eddie started out life as a character in a series of letters to my nephew Ben? Will there be yet more adventures one day? Come closer and I'll tell you . . . Closer . . . You'd better believe it! Until then, it's curtain up for *Final Curtain*. Quiet at the back there, please.

PHILIP ARDAGH
Ireland, 2006

Contents

Prologue

HARRY: That's the 'ouse.

THUNK: You sure?

HARRY: 'Course I'm sure!

THUNK: How comes you're so sure you're sure?

HARRY: How many other 'ouses d'you reckon have 'ollow cows in their flowerbeds?

THUNK: I was only askin', 'arry . . . Do we do the job tonight?

HARRY: 'Course we don't do the job tonight. Have you been listenin' to a word I've been tellin' you? We waits until the time is right.

THUNK: And 'ow do we know when that is?

HARRY: When our man on the inside says it is.

THUNK: You mean –?

HARRY: Correct. We're about to rob them Dickenses blind with a little 'elp from a viper in their own nest.

THUNK: Ha! Does that mean we can get out of this ditch now, 'arry?

HARRY: It most certainly does, Thunk. Let's be on our way.

Episode 1

Is This a Dagger?

*In which Eddie plays himself, and
Even Madder Aunt Maud acts true to form*

As the dagger was thrust towards Eddie Dickens a second time, he managed to throw himself clear, crashing down against a pile of barrels that rolled haphazardly across the bare-planked floor.

'There's no escape, my boy!' bellowed the knife-wielding masked man, looming above him, weapon poised and ready to strike.

'Stop that at once!' cried a voice, grating enough to peel the zest off a lemon at one-hundred-and-two paces, and the next thing the masked man knew was that he was being battered about the head with a stuffed stoat.

The actor-manager Mr Pumblesnook (for it was he in the costume of 'villain') had always tried to impress upon those under his tuition that, when performing, it was of the utmost – the *utmost* – importance to stay in character, no matter what.

Over the past few weeks at Awful End, however, he had learned to take this golden rule, hide it in a piece of sacking, slip it into a bottom drawer and forget ALL about it, when dealing with two particular people. Said people were Mad Mr Jack Dickens (*aka* Mad Uncle Jack, MUJ, or Mad Major Dickens) and his lovely wife, Even Madder Aunt Maud.

It was the latter who was beating the poor man about the head at that moment. 'My good lady,' said Mr Pumblesnook (as himself and not the villain). 'Might I remind you for the umpteenth time that I am not actually attacking your great-nephew. He and I are undertaking a dramatic endeavour. We are rehearsing a play –' He used his forearms and elbows to fend off the blows as best he could. '– as we were when you attacked me three times yesterday, twice the day before and on heaven-knows-how-many occasions on heaven-knows-how-many days prior to that.'

'So *you* say,' snapped Even Madder Aunt Maud. 'But how can I be sure that you're not really attacking him *this time*?'

'I'm fine, Aunt Maud,' said Eddie, who'd already got to his feet. 'We're only pretending.'

'PRETENDING?' boomed Mr Pumblesnook, his voice loud enough to deafen a passing earwig. (I have a sworn affidavit from the earwig to that effect, which is a kind of legal statement not commonly used in the insect world.) 'We are not pretending, Master Edmund. We are ACTING.'

Even Madder Aunt Maud thrust Malcolm's nose right up against Mr Pumblesnook's. Stuffed stoat and actor-manager eyed each other suspiciously. 'Don't shout at the boy,' she said.

Pumblesnook produced a flamboyant kerchief from the breast pocket of his purple jacket and mopped perspiration from his brow. (This sentence is now also available in English: He pulled out a hanky and wiped the sweat off his forehead.) 'Forgive me, dear lady, but my two most oft repeated reminders of these past few weeks are that I am NOT actually intending to harm the boy and, young Edmund, we are acting – thinking ourselves into living a part and being a character – and are not *pretending*.' He said this last word as though it were an unpleasant gas given off by an embarrassing-looking fungus.

'Sorry,' said Eddie.

'Particularly when, in this instance, the character you are playing is yourself.'

'A point well made, Mr Pumblesnook,' said Eddie for, in the play they were currently rehearsing, Eddie Dickens was indeed playing Eddie Dickens, the play being a dramatisation of certain episodes from his life. The dramatisation wasn't simply the telling of true events from Eddie's recent past; the playwright had decided that he should change the odd fact here and there to make it even more dramatic.

The playwright in question was none other than Eddie's own father, Mr Dickens, who had announced that 'writing can't be that difficult if that oaf Ardagh can do it.' The statement had been greeted with a few polite 'mmms', one 'surely' and an 'absolutely' because no-one had any idea who this Ardagh fellow he was referring to actually was.

It was once he was under way, with several piles of scrumpled paper, sleepless nights and ink-stained fingers later, that Mr Dickens had realised – as many had before him and have since – that one should *never* let the facts get in the way of a good story.

The scene Mr Pumblesnook and Eddie had been rehearsing when they'd been so rudely interrupted by EMAM (again) was one of a number set on board *The Pompous Pig* bound for America, where Eddie came face-to-face with the escaped convict, Swags (the true version of which is beautifully laid out in my book *Terrible Times*). Mr Pumblesnook was playing the role of Swags.

Those of you familiar with Eddie's earlier adventures may recall that Swags was a very thin man and Mr Pumblesnook a very large one. The reason for such miscasting was simple: as director and producer of the show, Mr Pumblesnook insisted on taking all the best parts for himself. At the initial casting, he had even tried to give himself the title role of Eddie but even he had to eventually admit that Eddie had been born to play the part.

Most of the other roles were played by Mr Pumblesnook's band of players, made up of the original core of actors Eddie had first encountered at the rather unoriginally named *The Coaching Inn* coaching inn plus those escaped orphans from St Horrid's Home for Grateful Orphans who'd chosen to stay with him after their escape.

In fact, the escape was the climax at the end of the first act. The real Marjorie, the hollow cow-shaped carnival float in which they'd escaped, was now Even Madder Aunt Maud's home in the rose garden of Awful End. In the play, it was portrayed by a much smaller two dimensional painted wooden cow on wheels.

Like most of the working props, these were constructed by one of the wandering theatricals, Mr Blessing. And, like most of the wandering theatricals, he had rather an annoying nickname: Bless Him. I'm sorry, but there it is.

For this play, Bless Him was ably assisted by Eddie's cousin, Fabian. Fabian would have made a fantastic understudy for Eddie because they looked so like each other that, when they weren't mistaken for each other they were mistaken for virtually identical twins. (Their eyes were somewhat different. More on this later.) When asked, however, Fabian had refused, point blank, to act. The conversation went something like this:

'You are aware that I am writing a play?'

'Yes, Uncle Laudanum.'

'Being an account of some of the more exciting moments in my son Edmund's disproportionately action packed life –'

'Yes, uncle.'

'– without the distractions and asides of –'

'Yes, uncle.'

'Well, Fabian, I was wondering whether you would consider being an understudy?'

'A basement?'

'I think you are confusing an understudy with an undercroft.'

'I'm sorry, uncle.'

'An understudy is someone who learns another person's part so, if that person is taken ill, he can take on the role in his place.'

'His part?'

'His character. His acting role in the play.'

'But I could never do that . . .'

'You would rather have a role all to yourself?'

'No, it's not that. It's just that I couldn't act in front of people.'

'These are not people, Fabian. They are family,

and a few close friends. Not *people*. The stage will be built here at Awful End and the play performed in the grounds.'

'Then perhaps I could help with that, uncle? With building the stage –?'

'And props! What an excellent idea.'

And so it was. As director and producer and manager and player of all the best parts other than Eddie's, Mr Pumblesnook was clearly in charge but he fully understood patronage. As well as his handsome fee, he was being housed and fed at Awful End, along with his acting troupe, and Mr Dickens had written the script himself. So Mr Dickens got listened to. Mr Dickens got respect. And his weird family, who were also his hosts, were reluctantly tolerated.

The member of the household – for want of a better description – with whom the actor-manager was on worst terms was Malcolm (or was it Sally?). Once, when disguised as a highwayman, Mr Pumblesnook had the misfortune of being hit across the knees with Malcolm – something *not* dramatised in the play – and he had never forgiven the stuffed stoat. This was, of course, totally unreasonable as Malcolm had no say in the matter and, in the improbable – nay impossible – situation where he might have had an opinion, he would, I've no doubt, have felt sorely wronged. It was

10

Even Madder Aunt Maud the man should have been angry with: it being she who'd used Malcolm as a weapon on him.

Mr Pumblesnook was holding Malcolm's nose in his grip right now, EMAM still clutching his tail end, or should that be 'the end of his tail'?

'Madam,' he said firmly, in a voice he'd used to such great effect when playing the Archbishop in *Steeple Chase*, 'if you would be so kind as to put that stoat away and go about your normal business, young Eddie and I shall do likewise.'

'But you don't have stoats to put away!' she snorted.

'The normal business, ma'am!' Mr Pumblesnook sighed, 'We shall likewise go about our normal business!'

Even Madder Aunt Maud went up on tiptoe and glared straight into the actor-manager's eyes. 'There's nothing normal about you, sir!' she declared, then turned and stomped off, waving Malcolm before her, like a commander leading his troops into battle, sword raised.

Mr Pumblesnook watched her go. 'Your great-aunt certainly knows how to make a grand exit, Eddie,' he said, almost grudgingly. There had been a time when he'd greatly admired her, but living in prolonged proximity to her had soon cured him of that. 'Now where were we?'

'You were about to take another stab at me with that dagger,' Eddie reminded him.

'Not I!' declared Pumblesnook, his voice rising. 'That villain Swags!' and, with that, he was back in character and chasing Eddie between the scattered barrels.

Episode 2

Goodbyes, Hellos & Tallyhos!

*In which we say goodbye to a bunch of monks
and get to know a bunch of relatives better*

Eddie had been sorry to see the monks go when they finally left Awful End. He felt good at having been able to return the favour and put them up when they were monastery-less, and now the place seemed very empty without them. Awful End was a vast house (and, following the success of these books, I've heard rumours that the current generation of the Dickens family are considering opening it to the public during the summer months, and then that way you'll be able to see for yourselves), so it could easily accommodate a few hundred monks. He would miss their company, their conversations, their chanting and singing.

With them gone, it was back to 'normal' – as if that term could be applied to Awful End – but with a few noticeable differences. Now there were also Eddie's newly-discovered Aunt Hester (whom everyone called Hetty), a newly-discovered uncle, called Alfie (who had a permanent hacking cough), and Eddie's newly-discovered cousins, Fabian and baby Oliphant, living with them.

As I touched upon in Episode One, Eddie and Fabian looked very similar indeed. In truth, *so* similar that when David Roberts came to illustrate this book he could have cheated and simply drawn Eddie twice – which, my American friends, is how we say 'two times' on this side of the Atlantic – then pointed at one at random and said, 'That one there is Fabian!' (Even professional illustrators employ tricks like that sometimes, you know.)

Despite their eyes being different colours, that wasn't the way most people told them apart (because, generally, people couldn't remember who had the brown ones and who had the greenly-blue ones). It was the fact that Eddie's looked more saucery that was the trick.

The reason why Eddie had such saucer-like eyes is a pretty safe bet. Few people, Fabian included, had experienced as many eye-opening events in his life as Eddie had. Everywhere Eddie turned, he seemed to find himself in extraordinary situation

14

after extraordinary situation (rather like those characters in TV murder mysteries who, wherever they go, always seem to stumble upon a dead body, week after week after week). It probably didn't help living with such an extraordinary family. And, oh yes, whilst I remember, Fabian wore a gold hoop earring in one ear.

Baby Oliphant looked pretty much like any other baby boy, which meant that Aunt Hetty thought that he was the most handsome baby ever born, and the others thought of him as being generally quite nice, apart from the dribbling. He seemed to love Fabian and Eddie in equal measure and cooed when they were around. Apart from his mother, though, Oliphant's favourite person in the whole wide world seemed to be ex-chambermaid (and now 'maid of all works') Gibbering Jane, which made her gibber with pleasure on pleasure-gibbering levels one would never have imagined possible. This is why I've drawn this graph:

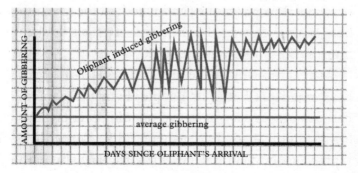

At every available opportunity, she would proudly wheel little Ollie around the grounds in a home-made pram (even though he was now a pretty fast crawler in his own right). As well as being able to say 'Mamma', 'Dadda' and 'narna' the last of which – I think – meant food, he could also do some impressive gibbering noises of his own, which Jane took as a real compliment.

And another noticeable difference at Awful End? Why, the arrival of Mr Pumblesnook's wandering theatricals, of course. Mad Uncle Jack hadn't initially liked the idea of the actors and actresses – female actors weren't called plain actors back then – staying in the house itself. In those days, in the great scheme of things, actors (and actresses) were seen to be below woodlice and earwigs in the hierarchy of living things . . . which might explain why he suggested that they each be issued with a large piece of tree bark to sleep under in the gardens. Mr Dickens had managed to persuade him that Awful End was so big and had so many empty rooms that he would hardly know they were there. When he pointed out that the monks had caused them very little inconvenience, and MUJ had replied, 'What monks?' he knew that he'd won. Mr Pumblesnook's troupe arrived and all was well.

Eddie was very pleased to see again so many of

the orphans he'd helped to escape, and to see how much better fed and happier they looked nowadays. And they were pleased to see him. Eddie Dickens would always be held in special regard by the former occupants of St Horrid's Home for Grateful Orphans.

Surprisingly, it was EMAM who seemed to miss the monks most of all, and this was expressed by the fact that she often mentioned how little she missed them. Or thought about them. Hardly ever.

'I won't miss the one with a face like a gargoyle,' said Even Madder Aunt Maud one sunny afternoon.

'Abbot Po was a very nice man,' said Eddie in his defence.

'Never said he wasn't, but he was ugly enough to stop all the clocks, and Ethel wouldn't lay,' snapped his great-aunt.

'Ethel?' asked Fabian.

It took Eddie a moment to remember about whom EMAM was talking. 'She means her favourite chicken . . . only it's no wonder she didn't lay any eggs while Abbot Po was here. She was dead and buried years ago.' (In fact, Ethel the chicken was buried long before a single Bertian monk set foot in Awful End.)

'That doesn't make my statement any less true!" snorted Even Madder Aunt Maud, bringing an axe crashing down over her head. Not on Eddie or Fabian, I hasten to add. I suppose I should have explained that they were in the woodshed, shouldn't I?

Though called a shed, it was more of a lean-to with the outer wall missing: a covered area where the logs for the fires were cut and stacked.

It used to be the ex-soldiers' job to cut the wood, but they were getting a bit past it now and had had rather too many accidents and near misses over more recent years. Dawkins had a bad back, so wood-chopping couldn't be included in his endless list of duties. The younger monks had loved chopping wood but now, of course, they'd gone.

Even Madder Aunt Maud had announced that it would now be one of her responsibilities. No sooner had the words passed her lips than an involuntary shudder had passed through Eddie's entire body. The thought of his great-aunt wielding a large axe seemed about as safe and sensible as appointing a piranha fish to be a lifeguard or asking a cat-burglar to clean your gutters. That's why Eddie and Fabian were out in the woodshed-that-wasn't-really-a-shed with her, at a safe distance. They wanted to make sure that she didn't do herself a serious injury.

Both boys were impressed how strong their great-aunt was. She wasn't a very tall lady but she was fit

18

and healthy (which was probably why she would go on to live to the ripe old age that she did).

It was as Even Madder Aunt Maud was just about to narrowly miss chopping off the toes of her right foot by the narrowest of narrow margins for the third time that a bugle sounded.

Those of you with an army background might think of the sounding of a bugle as a call to get up in the morning, or to go to the cookhouse, or to fight, or to remember the dead – a bugle has a surprising number of uses in army life doesn't it? – and, if you're a lover of boogie (as in music), the sound of the bugle may remind you of the *Boogie-Woogie Bugle Boy of Company B*, a song made famous by the singing group The Andrews Sisters, not to be confused with the Andrews sisters (small 's') who lived in Lamberley Hall (not too far from Awful End) and owned one of the finest collections of reject china in the British Empire at the time, which included three-handled two-handled mugs (if you see what I mean), some of the finest sets of chipped or incomplete dinner and tea services, and soup bowls so warped that they couldn't hold soup.

The sisters, Kitty and Amelia Andrews, had inherited the Hall from their father, the Honourable Douglas 'Duff' Andrews, (who was 'new money', having made his fortune from coconuts), and neither had ever married.

They had little to do with the outside world and spent so much of the time just speaking to each other that they'd fallen into the habit of knowing exactly what the other was going to say, so rarely needed to speak complete sentences. A typical Andrews sisters' (with a small 's') conversation might go along the lines of:

'Do you know where –?'

'Under the –'

'How on earth –?'

'I hid them from –'

'Wise move!'

which, once translated, would read:

KITTY: Do you know where I put the scissors?
AMELIA: Under the sofa.
KITTY: How on earth did they get there?
AMELIA: I hid them from Cleptomania Claire.
KITTY: Wise move!
JULIE: *The hills are alive with the sound of –*

I'm *so* sorry. I've no idea how Julie Andrews ended up in the mix. That's certainly one Andrews too many . . . and do please remind me: how did I get on to the Andrews sisters (with a small 's') in the first place?

Let me work backwards: Andrews sisters (with a small 's') > Andrews Sisters (with a big 'S') > *The Boogie-Woogie Bugle Boy from Company B* > bugles > Even Madder Aunt Maud, Fabian and Eddie in the woodshed, hearing a bugle sounding. Aha! Here we are:

Though the sound of a bugle may mean different things to different people, a bugle sounding here at Awful End meant one thing: the local fox hunt.

Mad Uncle Jack had banned fox hunting on his land, though it had little to do with the fox. A man who paid for everything with dried (dead) fish probably wasn't overly concerned with the foxes' wellbeing. The reason why Mad Uncle Jack (or Mad Mr Jack Dickens or Mad Major Jack Dickens, as he was known locally) had banned it was because he was in dispute with the Master of the Hounds (who was the chap in charge of the local hunt).

This chap was another retired major but, unlike MUJ, who'd reverted to plain 'Mr' now that his fighting days were over, Stinky Hoarebacker still used his military title. Of course, he wasn't christened 'Stinky'. His first name was actually Cheshire, which is also the name of a type of cheese and, if you share your name with a type of cheese and you go to an English public school – which, dear American readers, is what we English call our *private* schools for some unknown reason – there is a 98.6% chance that you're going to end up being called 'Stinky' for the rest of your natural born days.

He and Mad Uncle Jack had fallen out over a bet. A few years prior to the events I'm now relating – sometime between those outlined in *Terrible Times* and *Dubious Deeds*, I think – Mad Uncle Jack and Stinky Hoarebacker had been discussing hats. Mad Uncle Jack had insisted that the deerstalker was the finest hat of its generation. Stinky had insisted that it was the mullion.

'What *are* you talking about?' MUJ had demanded, tightening the strap under his saddle. I'm sure such straps have special names and, being the horsey type, my editor might even point it out to me and suggest we add it here. In other words, if you read this paragraph *without* the technical name for such a piece of tackle added, then it's probably because she's not doing her job properly. 'The mullion is a cap, not a hat!'

'It is most certainly not,' Stinky had insisted.

At this moment, Mad uncle Jack snorted. 'The finest of hats is the deerstalker, the mullion is a cap and not a hat, and there's an end to it,' he whinnied.

'It most certainly is a hat, sir!' replied Stinky.

'It most certainly is *not*, sir!' MUJ retorted, which isn't as painful as it sounds.

''Tis, sir!'

'*Not*, sir!'

''Tis! 'Tis! 'Tis!'

''Tisn't! 'Tisn't! 'Tisn't!'

'A wager?' which is a bet, suggested Stinky.

'A wager!' which is still a bet, agreed Mad Uncle Jack. 'What will it be?'

'A shilling!' which is an amount of money, suggested Stinky.

'Done, sir!' said MUJ. 'I'll wager you one shilling, sir, that the mullion is not, was not, and never shall be a hat. It's a *cap*.'

The two retired majors shook hands. Mad Uncle Jack then instructed that the local hunt not be permitted in the grounds of Awful End, and the two men had not spoken to each other since . . . yet the bugle had sounded and here came the hunt. And Even Madder Aunt Maud was ready for them!

Episode 3

A Cracking Time

*In which an enemy is vanquished
and we welcome a new arrival*

'Battle stations!' cried Mad Aunt Maud, not to be confused with Battle Station which is a railway station between Crowhurst and Robertsbridge on the Hastings to London line. (It was at Battle and not Hastings that the Battle of Hastings took place, but it wasn't called Battle – the place, not the fighting – until *after* the event, of course.) She threw the axe to the ground, snatching her stuffed stoat off the pile of stacked logs where she'd positioned him to 'watch' what she was doing.

24

The huntsmen didn't stand a chance. I won't go into details as to how she got them off the Dickens estate, but I will say that some of Even Madder Aunt Maud's victims smelled of bats' urine for a good few days after that (despite regular bathing) and, of those who fell down the freshly dug pits, only three had broken bones.

As for the fox, it's far from clear as to whether they were actually chasing one. There was some talk in the local villages about Stinky Hoarebacker setting the dogs on a foreign brush salesman – both the salesman and the brushes being foreign – who, unfamiliar with British ways, had made the unforgivable error of knocking on the retired major's *front* door, rather than trying his luck at the tradesmen's entrance around the back.

Either way, the huntsmen were repelled, and the senior members of the Dickens family felt triumphant in victory. (Even the younger actors had been enlisted to help. The ex-St Horrid's orphans particularly enjoyed themselves, some even wielding cucumbers, evoking memories of the old days.) Fabian was a little overwhelmed by it all. He still found it difficult to adjust to life at Awful End. It wasn't just that, having been brought up amongst travelling gypsies, he was used to forever being on the move, but also had to do with the fact that he found his recently discovered relatives – er – a little eccentric. Oh, all right: he found them CRAZY.

I'm not sure of the derivation of the word 'crazy', and I don't have an ordinary dictionary to hand, because I'm living out of boxes at the moment. (More on this later, no doubt.) What I *do* have is *Old Roxbee's Dictionary of Architecture & Landscape Architecture* (in the revised edition of 1972, long after *Old Roxbee* had become *So-Old-He's-Long-Since-Dead Roxbee*). According to this, 'crazy paving' – the nearest thing I can get to the word 'crazy' on its own – is so called because it's made up of cracked paving stones seemingly laid without order . . . which is a pretty good description of the majority of the members of the Dickens family at the time: cracked and orderless. By comparison, Fabian's family was very normal. His mother behaved like a loving mother, glad to be recognised by her blood relatives at long last. Baby Oliphant behaved like a baby Oliphant, rather than, say, a baby elephant.* His father, Alfie, behaved like anyone with a bad cough: coughing badly, a great deal.

* For those of you've who've been waiting for an elephant joke ever since we discovered that the baby's real name was Oliphant, your wait is over.

Poor Alfie Grout had one of those coughs that sounded so rough you could imagine it sand-papering his innards every time it started, but it also had a strange rattle that suggested he was far from well. One minute he'd be having a pleasant conversation about the annual gypsy horse fair over in Garlington Wake, and the next minute he'd be bent double coughing and rattling with a pained expression on his face.

This caused different reactions from different members of the Dickens household. Fabian would politely ignore it, because his father had told him to. Oliphant would dribble and coo. (That was his job, being a baby.) Fabian's mother would put a sympathetic arm around her husband and offer words of encouragement. Eddie would offer to get him a glass of water. Gibbering Jane would gibber. Dawkins, the gentleman's gentleman, would await instructions. Mrs Dickens would urge him to try stuffing his mouth with something . . . *anything*. Mr Dickens would hurriedly hold a handkerchief up to his *own* face for fear of catching something (usually muttering 'If Ardagh gives this hacking cough to anyone else, it's bound to be me!', whatever that meant). Which leaves Mad Uncle Jack and his lovely wife Even Madder Aunt Maud. Mad Uncle Jack would usually give Alfie a hearty slap on the back with a cheery, 'That's the spirit!', whilst EMAM was more likely to beat him with Malcolm with an 'Oh, do be quiet!'. Interestingly, it was these last two approaches that seemed to have the best effect on poor Alfie, short-term at least. Which only goes to show something, but I'm not exactly sure what.

Hang on? What's this? I've just noticed an old dictionary up on that shelf there, by the battered box of *Scrabble* and something called *Kerplunk*. This isn't my house so I had no way of knowing that there'd be one so readily to hand. Excuse me a moment. I can look up 'crazy' after all. *Craggy* . . . *cram* . . . *crambo* . . . *CRAMBO?* . . . apparently that's a game in which a player says a word for which the others must find a rhyme . . . *craw* . . . *crayfish* . . . *crazy*. Here we are! 'Unbalanced . . . absurdly out of place . . .' And, chiefly in North America – as opposed to a North American chief – *crazies* with an 'i' are crazy people. Not to be confused with *crazes*, without the 'i', which refers to widespread but short-lived enthusiasms for collecting brightly coloured plastic things, or wearing weird clothes which look very silly and outdated in next to no time.

So, there you are. How did I get onto this? I'm not sure, so let's pause for a picture of me in my current surroundings, then return to the main action.

Lovely. (Do you think my new glasses suit me?)

★

The family were gathered in the library. Eddie loved this room. There were books here, there and everywhere, and in places where there weren't books, there were things made to *look* like books. For example, when the doors were closed it was difficult to see them at first glance because they too were built to look like shelves of books. In Eddie's day, books in a such a fine library were leather-bound with the title (and sometimes author) embossed on the brown leather spines with gold lettering. Even the fake wooden book spines on the doors were embossed in this way to create the illusion of uninterrupted shelving all the way around the walls. The only spaces were for the windows but, when it was dark out, wooden shutters could be folded across them and on these were painted yet more book spines.

Though there has been a library, of sorts, for as long as Awful End has stood on that spot, it was Eddie's great-grandfather – in other words, Mr Dickens's grandfather and Mad Uncle Jack's father – Dr Malcontent Dickens who had turned the library into this splendid room. Malcontent Dickens (whose full name was Malcontent Arthur Rigmarole Dickens) was a great lover of knowledge, or 'nolidge' as he called it, spelling not being his greatest forte, and believed (rightly) that much knowledge could be gleaned from books.

The Dickens family had expected great things of Malcontent and he had achieved great things but, sadly, not longevity. He was untimely killed by a human cannonball. It was an accident, and need not distract us here. Eddie's grandfather, Percy Dickens, had inherited the love of books from his father, but not Awful End, which eventually ended up in Mad Uncle Jack's hands. Jack had little time for books but, fortunately, didn't decide to flood the library to make a fish tank (which the eldest brother, George, had considered doing), or to use the books to build his tree house.

So here they all were, in the library, on the evening that Stinky Hoarebacker's fox hunt had been repelled from the estate in shambolic retreat.

'Congratulations are in order!' said Mad Uncle Jack, raising a glass of sherry high above his head. It hit a light fitting and shattered.

'In order of what?' demanded Even Madder Aunt Maud. She was still wearing a camouflage hat made of laurel leaves which she'd used to sneak up close on her targets. Her original plan had been to bite the horses' legs so that they'd rear up and throw their riders. Then, she'd reasoned that it wasn't the horses' fault – they were just doing what they were supposed to do – so she'd bitten the riders instead. 'In order of age? Size?'

'In whatever order you like, my fountain of love!' said Mad Uncle Jack, in a voice he reserved for speaking to his beloved wife. He was dusting the tiny sticky shards of broken sherry schooner (glass) from what little hair he had. 'You choose!' said Even Madder Aunt Maud.

'Then I choose congratulations in any old order!' announced MUJ.

The others raised their glasses and drank, but not until they'd lowered them and put them to their lips. You try drinking with a glass raised above your head. It's not easy.

Their celebration was interrupted by a sudden outbreak of gibbering which, as the brighter sparks amongst you will have guessed, was caused by

Gibbering Jane. She ran into the library, the singed piece of knitted tea-cosy she always wore on a string around her neck, trailing out behind her, like a scarf on a windy day. She was clutching an enormous egg with both hands. It appeared to be cracking.

'It's hatching!' she yelped, before resuming her more usual senseless gibbering. The room was galvanised, which is a strange phrase when you come to think about it. A galvanised bucket is a bucket coated in a protective layer of zinc using electricity (named after the Italian psychologist Luigi Galvani, who's probably better known for using electricity to make dead frogs' legs twitch . . . perhaps having nothing better to do.) A galvanised room is – in this case, at least – when the people in the room were excited – yippee! – into action.

Everyone put their drinks down, except for Even Madder Aunt Maud who simply let hers fall to the floor, narrowly avoiding a library chair, (which could be folded out to form a ladder to reach some of the books on the shelves at mid-height). The glass bounced on a rug woven into the shape of the Baltic States by a distant cousin of Eddie's mother, spilling its contents without breaking.

Maud snatched the egg. 'Mine, I believe,' she said, which was true enough. The egg had been a gift from the Head of Aviaries at The Royal

Zoological Institute in Kemphill Park (not to be confused with the Royal Zoological Gardens in Regent's Park, which later became better known as Regent's Park Zoo and then, even more recently, as plain old London Zoo.)

The Head of Aviaries at The Royal Zoological Institute, a certain Dr Marcus Loach, wasn't in the habit of giving away eggs to almost total strangers, but it was by way of an apology for what had happened to EMAM during a recent visit to the zoo.

Dr Loach had been under the impression that Even Madder Aunt Maud was a member of a group of visiting foreign dignitaries with a particular interest in zoology, who had suffered an unfortunate accident whilst under his care. Little did he realise that the woman clutching the stuffed stoat was simply tagging along. (The foreign dignitaries assumed that she was a member of staff – possibly in charge of small mammals, by the looks of the rather strange creature she was holding.) She had, in truth, forced her way through a hole in the hedge to the wilderbeast enclosure whilst on what we today might call 'a fungus foray' (in other words, looking for mushrooms).

As for the accident, she hadn't fallen into the crocodile enclosure (as Loach had assumed) but had deliberately climbed over the railings and into the water to get nearer to the single croc occupying it which, she later told her doting husband, 'gave me a warm feeling as it reminded me of one of my dear late mother's handbags.'

She was just about to introduce Malcolm to said crocodile, which was observing her movements with a seemingly indifferent gaze through a half-closed eye (whilst, in all probability, actually sizing her up as a potential pre-lunchtime snack), when she was spotted by what, today, we'd call a zoo keeper. Without a moment's thought for his own safety the man, a Mr Johnson, dived into the pea-soup coloured water and dragged a protesting Even Madder Aunt Maud to safety, receiving a mouthful of algae and several blows from a stuffed stoat for his trouble.

Dr Marcus Loach, whose job it had been to escort the dignitaries throughout the day, though birds were his area of expertise, was mortified (which may sound as if it has something to do with the lime, cement, sand and water mix used to bond bricks together, but, in the case of Dr Loach, meant embarrassed and humiliated). The whole reason he'd been entrusted with the task of showing these important folk about the place was because the Director of The Royal Zoological Institute in Kemphill Park was grooming him as his successor.

When monkeys groom each other, it usually involves carefully going through each other's hair, removing ticks and bugs and eating them. This was certainly not the way that Sir Trevor Hartley-Poole behaved towards Dr Loach. He was simply preparing the younger – though not young – man for the role. This was excellent news for Dr Loach for he knew that, on Hartley-Poole's recommendation, he would become the new director unopposed. A visiting VIP being almost eaten by a crocodile would *not* be the kind of thing to impress Sir Trevor, hence Loach's feeling of mortification.

Dr Loach had to think quickly. He sent the

heroic Mr Johnson to change out of his wet clothes and to have the afternoon off, on the strict understanding that he say nothing to anyone about the incident, hinting that his silence may well result in his promotion to Keeper of the Queen's Giraffe (which was one of the most sort-after jobs in the institute). He gave the crocodile an extra large lunch (to make up for not having eaten EMAM). And, as for Even Madder Aunt Maud, he took the unusual step of offering her a little something for her collection. (All the dignitaries had animal collections of varying sorts. That's why Sir Trevor Hartley-Poole had instructed Dr Loach to show them around the zoo in the first place.)

'Perhaps an egg?' Dr Loach had suggested, as they entered the aviary, his stoat-carrying guest having refused the offer of dry clothes. She simply squelched after the others, seemingly unconcerned by her terrible ordeal.

'Any egg?' she asked.

'Indeed, madam,' said Dr Loach.

Even Madder Aunt Maud hurried off and, ten minutes or so later, returned – somehow looking even damper than before, if that were possible – with an egg which, despite his vast knowledge of birds, the Head of Aviaries failed to identify.

'How about this one?' she asked.

'Consider it yours,' he said.

And now, after Gibbering Jane had lavished all the attention on it that she'd lavished on baby Oliphant when Eddie had found him in the bulrushes and named him Ned, the egg was hatching in the library of Awful End. Out popped a crocodile.

Episode 4

Doctor! Doctor!

*In which Annabelle snaps,
and Dawkins almost does*

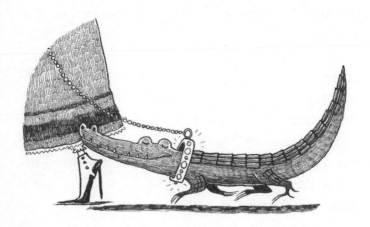

It soon became a common sight for Even Madder Aunt Maud to be followed around the house and gardens of Awful End by a tiny crocodile on a silver chain. She had removed the steps which led up into Marjorie (her hollow-cow home in the rose garden, as I've already mentioned) and replaced them with a ramp that Annabelle – the name she'd given the baby croc – could easily climb up and down. The work was carried out by Mad Uncle Jack's band of loyal ex-soldiers, so took up a ridiculous amount of time and wood.

At the centre of the rose garden lay a shallow rectangular pond, which was ideal for Annabelle to splash about in.

Although Even Madder Aunt Maud was even more eccentric than your average Victorian lady of the well-to-do classes, I should point out that the keeping of exotic pets was not unheard of. There was a chap called the Marquis of Queensberry who came up with the rules for boxing (which must be why they're called the Marquis of Queensberry Rules), and he had a sister whose married name was Lady Florence Dixie. Lady Florence had a pet puma, which she used to take for walks in Windsor Great Park. So perhaps EMAM's crocodile on a chain wasn't quite so utterly ridiculous as you at first imagined, hmmm, clever-clogs?!

Eddie and Fabian were fascinated by their great-aunt's new pet and offered to take her for walks between the endless play rehearsals. EMAM was reluctant to let anyone else but Gibbering Jane (who'd kept the egg warm, remember) look after her new special friend.

For a failed chambermaid who'd spent her life under the stairs at Eddie's previous home, before it was burnt to the ground, Jane was now very much in demand. Oliphant really loved her, and EMAM was regularly entrusting Annabelle to her care. Eddie had never seen her so happy.

Even Madder Aunt Maud took to having a crocodile around in her stride. Though obviously still fond of him, it did seem that living, breathing Annabelle had rather taken over from tatty, stuffed Malcolm as her Number One companion. Shocking, I know, but true.

Mad Uncle Jack hardly seemed to register that his wife now had a croc in tow. He slept in his tree house at night, and she slept in her hollow cow, with Annabelle at the foot of her bed, so that wasn't a problem.

Eddie's father, Mr Dickens, seemed a little concerned about there being a little crocodile about the place, pointing out that it would soon grow to be a *big* crocodile about the place, and possibly less friendly. But his complaints were half-hearted. His mind was on his *magnum opus*s which, in this instance, meant his play.

The person who was the least happy about there now being a many-toothed reptile in their lives was the member of the household who got bitten the most often, and that was Dawkins.

The first time the animal had bitten him was when Even Madder Aunt Maud had instructed him to pick Annabelle up and place her in the sink. This Dawkins had done without protest, and had received a little nip for his trouble. Thereafter, Annabelle would bite him at every available opportunity, which was why the gentleman's gentleman would often try to hide if he saw Even Madder Aunt Maud and Annabelle heading his way.

Once, Mr Pumblesnook's wife (the truly dreadful Mrs Pumblesnook) came upon Dawkins cowering in a very large silver-plated soup tureen. He claimed that he was cleaning it, but he could see that the actor-manager's wife was far from convinced.

Another time, he hid from Annabelle the baby croc in a large wicker basket in the laundry room. Unfortunately, his bad back seized up and it was two days before he was discovered by Bless Him, who'd been looking for some old shirts and longjohns to turn into sails for the stage representation of *The Pompous Pig*.

41

Like a goat, Annabelle seemed to eat anything and everything. Fabian took great delight in tossing her a whole lettuce or a cabbage and watching her snap it up. Once, he kicked a cabbage to her like a ball. The cabbage veered off in completely the wrong direction, but his shoe came flying off his foot and landed in the pond next to her, with a satisfying splash. Annabelle had eaten it before Gibbering Jane, who was sitting at the water's edge, could stop her.

'Ooops!' said Fabian, who thereafter hobbled around with just one shoe until he 'borrowed' a spare pair of Eddie's just before bed.

He and Eddie got on surprisingly well, in fact, and it was obvious that Eddie was delighted to have someone his own age – and *normal* – in his life! Eddie wasn't used to a child taking his stuff without asking but that was a small price to pay for having an ally in a household full of odd adults. And he was really enjoying this acting lark too. All in all, life was good.

Then Uncle Alfie's health took on a turn for the worse. As well as his appalling cough, his whole chest now felt tight and it was painful to lie down. He had to sleep in a sitting position with plenty of pillows packed around him.

'I think we need the doctor,' said Aunt Hetty at breakfast.

'Muffin or Humple?' asked Mr Dickens.

'A doctor,' repeated a puzzled Hetty, thinking she was being offered something to eat.

'They are both doctors, Aunt Hetty,' Eddie explained. 'Dr Humple is the family doctor and Dr Muffin a specialist.'

'He cured us when we became crinkly around the edges and smelled of old hot-water bottles,' said Mrs Dickens.

'What do old hot-water bottles smell like?' asked Hetty, thinking of her own hot-water bottle, an earthenware cylinder with a cork stopper in it.

'Like we did when we were ill,' said Mr Dickens.

'Then perhaps Dr Humple would be the better choice. Your Dr Muffin sounds very specialised,' Aunt Hetty reasoned.

'If I might interject, madam?' said Dawkins, who usually left the Dickenses and Grouts to serve themselves from the side table (on which he'd place various dishes under silver domes, in order to keep the food warm).

'What is it, Daphne?' asked Eddie's father.

'It's just that Mrs Grout –' he was referring to Hetty, of course '– might make a more informed decision if she was aware of the fact that Dr Humple is no more.'

'No more, what?' demanded Even Madder Aunt Maud, surfacing from her hiding place under the breakfast table. She'd been tying the men's shoe laces together whilst eavesdropping on the conversation. 'No more than a man with a funny hat and a stethoscope? No more than ninety-eight per cent water?'

'Dead, madam,' said Dawkins. 'He is alive no more.'

'He seemed perfectly alive the last time I saw him!' Even Madder Aunt Maud snorted.

'That's because he *was* indeed alive on that occasion, madam,' said Dawkins. 'He has died since.'

'I'm very sorry to hear that,' said Mr Dickens.

44

'How did he die? Do you know, Daphne?'

'Peacefully in his sleep, apparently, sir,' said Dawkins. 'He was seventy-two.'

'Er, has he a replacement, do you know?' asked Hetty, feeling it slightly indelicate to be discussing someone taking over the doctor's practice, but she needed someone to see her poor Alfie as soon as possible.

'I believe a Dr Moot has stepped in to care for his patients, and intends to take over his medical practice, madam,' said Dawkins, pleased to be the fount of all knowledge.

'Moot?' said Mad Aunt Maud, pulling herself upright with the aid of the tablecloth, causing it to slip across the table top and various items – such as knives and forks – to clatter to the floor. 'Not Moo-Cow Moot?'

'Madam?' asked Dawkins, with a what-on-Earth-are-you-on-about expression on his face.

'Old Mooty, huh?' Mad Uncle Jack joined in. 'It must be the same fella. There can't be that many Dr Moots knocking about the place.'

'I believe that his first name is Samuel, sir,' said Dawkins.

'That's him!' said MUJ, folding his paper and tossing it onto the table.

'The very same!' said EMAM. 'Samuel Moo-Cow Moot!'

'Will that be all?' Dawkins asked the assembled company. He had been summoned to the breakfast room by the bell, and was eager to get back to his sheets of tissue paper, which he was busy sorting in the pantry.

'Yes, thank you, Daphne, just bring those extra sausages we asked for,' said Mr Dickens. Dawkins bowed and backed out of the room.

By now, Even Madder Aunt Maud had found an empty chair at the table. She sat between Fabian and Eddie. 'Which one are you?' she asked Eddie.

'I'm Eddie, Mad Aunt Maud,' he said.

'I do wish you'd stop it!' she said.

Eddie had no idea what she was talking about.

'Is Dr Moot a good doctor?' Hetty interjected.

'Strange fellow,' said Mad Uncle Jack. 'He shot me once.'

'He shot you?' gasped Eddie.

'Yes. When I say once, he actually shot me twice, but on the one single occasion.'

'But why, uncle?' asked Hetty.

'He deserved it!' said Even Madder Aunt Maud. She had somehow managed to get Malcolm's snout stuck in a pot of marmalade shaped like an orange.

'Absolutely,' agreed MUJ. 'I mean to say, I'd have shot old Moo-Cow if he hadn't shot me first!'

'Was it a duel?' said Eddie, in growing wonder.

46

'It most certainly was, young Edmund!'

'What were you fighting about?' asked Fabian.

'It was before I was married to your lovely great-aunt,' said Mad Uncle Jack looking across the table to his beloved Maud. The expression on his face was so soppy that it would have put a big-eyed puppy dog to shame. 'Moo-Cow was as in love with her as I was and thought that I had insulted her good name.'

Eddie found it hard to imagine anyone being in love with his great-aunt – except for Mad Uncle Jack, of course – and her ever having had a good name which anyone could insult.

'He accused my love pumpkin of having called me ridiculous –' began Even Madder Aunt Maud.

'Which, of course, you are!' said Mad Uncle Jack.

'Precisely!' agreed Maud. Having successfully freed Malcolm's snout from the pot, she was busy licking the marmalade from his matted fur.

'So why did you fight the duel, Mad Uncle Jack?' Eddie asked.

'Because Moot had challenged me to one. It would not have been gentlemanly to decline!'

'I thought duels were illegal?' said Eddie's mother, who'd been silent until now because her mouth had been filled with buttons. (She later admitted that she'd cut them from Eddie's father's clothes, when his trousers fell down.) She would have preferred button mushrooms but, in her opinion, these were the next best thing.

'The law was different back then . . . or less rigorously followed, anyhow,' said MUJ.

'Where were you shot?' asked Mr Dickens, who'd never heard this particular family anecdote before, nor noticed any scars.

'Near *The Eel*.'

'The eel?' said Mr Dickens, imagining a place near the spleen.

'The coaching inn near Little Gattling,' said Mad Uncle Jack. He might have said more, but Dawkins burst into the room and burst into tears.

'I'm not sure how much more of this I can take, madam!' he sobbed, facing Even Madder Aunt Maud. One of the sausages he was carrying, piled high on a serving dish, fell to the floor with a dull thud.

'What *are* you on about?' she demanded.

The gentleman's gentleman turned to reveal that Annabelle the baby crocodile had attached herself to his bottom with her teeth.

Episode 5

Surprising News

*In which Mad Uncle Jack
receives an offer he can't refuse*

Back in Eddie's era, there were numerous postal deliveries in a day. At my home, there's one delivery and it's sometime in the morning. That sometime is usually when I'm in the bath, or changing a nappy or in the middle of an important phone call or jotting down a brilliant idea . . . and the postman invariably knocks because someone has invariably sent me something too large to fit through my letterbox: a rolled up poster, a big book, or a fan letter wrapped around a bar of gold bullion (*hint hint*). He never seems to come when I'm eagerly waiting for mail or *not* in the middle of something else.

At Awful End, at the time that the events I'm recounting in this third and final Further Adventure occurred, there was definitely an early morning post, a late morning post, a midday post, and an early afternoon post. There may also possibly have been a late afternoon post, but I'm not prepared to swear to it on a stack of Bibles. (I might fall off.) On this particular morning, when Eddie's Aunt Hetty was trying to find a doctor for his poor Uncle Alfie, the morning post brought an innocent enough sounding letter which was, eventually, to throw the house into utter turmoil (not to be confused with Upper Turnall which was a small hamlet not a stone's throw from Awful End, if one was extremely good at throwing stones*).

The letter, when it arrived, lay on the oval table in the centre of the hall, directly beneath the truly dreadful ceiling painted by Eddie's father, Mr

* Not that you should throw stones, whether you live in a glass house or not.**

** My editor has pointed out that there are already a great many footnotes in this adventure, which is nice because I thought she'd dozed off. I pointed out that in the UK editions of all the previous Eddie Dickens books, the only one to contain a footnote was *Awful End*, and that was only one, single note . . . which means that I've got a lot of catching up to do.

Dickens, which – though supposedly depicting a biblical scene – left the vast majority of onlookers with a queasy liver-sausagey feeling (though it wasn't quite as dreadful as Mrs Pumblesnook).

Fortunately, said letter had been picked up by Hetty who, suddenly remembering that it was in her pocket, produced it at the breakfast table and handed it to Mad Uncle Jack. I say 'fortunately' because, had EMAM picked it up, she might have absent-mindedly fed it to Annabelle, or posted it through a crack in the plasterwork in the wall by a piece of furniture referred to as the hall stand.

Mad Uncle Jack took the letter and tore open the envelope. In his younger days, there had been no such thing as envelopes, people simply used to fold over their letters when finishing them, write a name and address on the blank side and seal them shut with sealing wax. Some men wore signet rings which they pressed into the wax when it was hot to leave an impression of their family crest, or monogram, so that the person receiving the letter would know who it was from before they'd even opened it.

A cygnet – same pronunciation, different spelling – is the name for a baby swan but, I'm delighted to report that, as mad as the pair of them were, neither Mad Uncle Jack nor Even Madder Aunt Maud ever tried to use a swan (baby or adult) to leave an impression on sealing wax, either accidentally or on purpose (or accidentally on purpose); though they did once try to make an impression on the local bishop with a Christmas goose, but that's quite a different matter.

This letter, however, came in an envelope and hadn't required sealing wax to keep it shut. Mad Uncle Jack scanned the page with his eyes. 'Ridiculous!' he said.

'How so, uncle?' asked Mr Dickens.

'The buffoon who composed this confounded letter has written the entire thing upside down.'

Immediately to his right, Even Madder Aunt Maud emerged from under the table. She'd grown tired of sitting between the two boys and had resumed her position on the floor.

She snatched the letter from Mad Uncle Jack's

hand, turned it the right way up and handed it back to him.

Eddie was stunned. To him it was like a dog suddenly speaking the Queen's English, or a weeping willow tree stepping out of its bark and running, naked and giggling, into a lake for a swim. Even Madder Aunt Maud doing something *sensible*? That made no sense at all.

'You are a triumph!' said MUJ, kissing his wife on the back of her head with his thinnest of thin lips. In truth, they were his *only* lips – his only lips being thinnest of thin. (I don't wish to imply that he had a *fat* pair nestling alongside the dried swordfish he was inclined to carry around in his inside jacket pocket.) The thinnest comparison is with other people-with-thin-lips' lips, not with any other lips MUJ might himself have had.

'Sloppy characterisation,' muttered Eddie's father, to no one in particular.

'I'm sorry, dear?' asked Eddie's mother.

'One of us suddenly acting out of character, simply to move events along. This –' He stopped. Everyone was looking at him blankly. 'Never mind,' he sighed.

'Ha!' said MUJ, and it was such a *Ha!* that he had everyone's attention, including Annabelle's, who was now back on her silver chain behind EMAM, Dawkins's posterior having been successfully extricated from her pincer-like grip.

'What is it, uncle?' asked Fabian's mother. 'Not bad news, I hope?'

'My portrait,' said Mad Uncle Jack. 'The War Office wish to commission an oil painting of me, in full military regalia, to hang in Whitehall!'

'–' said Mr Dickens (which meant 'I'm at a loss for words').

'–' said Eddie (which meant, 'I don't know what to say').

'–' said Mrs Dickens (which meant she'd just bitten her tongue). Distressed by Alfie's turn for the worse in the coughing department, she had now filled her mouth with cleaning crystals from the sideboard*.

Mad Uncle Jack's news was quite extraordinary: *extraordinarily* extraordinary, in fact. Mad Major Jack Dickens's final military campaign had been an utter disaster. He would probably have ended up shooting some of his own men by mistake – or doing himself a personal injury – if his quick-witted batman (not a caped crusading superhero, but a soldier from the lower ranks whose job it was to act as a kind of gentleman's not-so-gentlemanly gentleman) hadn't removed all ammunition from

* If I knew what cleaning crystals were, I'd explain in a footnote right here.

MUJ's vicinity, and stuffed his rifle full of blotting paper.

Mad Uncle Jack's appalling record as a soldier was no great secret, hence the stunned silence. Why on Earth – or any other planet, come to that – would the War Office want someone to paint a portrait of Mad Uncle Jack and hang it at their headquarters in Whitehall?

'Marvellous!' cried Even Madder Aunt Maud. 'They probably need it to cover a damp patch.'

'It is, indeed, a great honour!' said MUJ.

'Congratulations, uncle,' said Mr Dickens.

'I wonder who they'll commission to paint it?' said Eddie.

'They mention the chap's name here,' said Mad Uncle Jack, referring back to the letter. 'Someone called A. C. Pryden. I can never abide a fellow who uses initials instead of a name –'

'He's very famous, uncle,' said Mr Dickens, who still fancied himself as a bit of an artist. 'I believe he painted General Gordon.'

'What colour?' snorted Even Madder Aunt Maud. 'Purple, I hope?' Eddie's great-aunt had recently developed an abiding passion for purple having seen a chromolithograph plate of a Roman emperor sporting a purple toga.

'I think he also painted Lord Bulberry,' said Eddie.

55

'Lazy n'er do well!' said EMAM waving Malcolm dangerously above her head.

'Lord Bulberry?' asked Hetty.

'This painter man . . . too lazy to use his full name!'

Today – I don't mean Tuesday (the day I'm writing this particular paragraph) but nowadays – Lord Bulberry is best-remembered (by those few who remember him at all) for having written *Surviving Three Years Down A Hole* and having invented a pocket knife with a particularly powerful spring. Back at the time of these events, though, he was known as the 'Hero of Guldoon', Guldoon being a place under siege. He defended Guldoon in some far off war against some far-off enemy until the British cavalry both physically and metaphorically arrived. It was the big news event of the year in Britain, and there were even celebrations in the street. To be painted by the same artist who captured Lord Bulberry on canvas was, indeed, an honour (if totally undeserved in MUJ's case).*

With Mad Uncle Jack and Even Madder Aunt Maud spending much of their time, and every

---

* It was later in life that his lordship began to miss the isolation of a besieged town, and so took to living down a hole for three years, only coming out to eat four square meals a day or to have a wash and a shave, and to sleep, of course.

night, in their treehouse made from creosoted dried fish and hollow wooden cow carnival float respectively, Eddie's mother had assumed the role as (almost) lady of the house, and was suddenly concerned where Pryden the painter would sleep if he came to stay at Awful End whilst painting his subject. It wasn't that there was a shortage of rooms – Mr Pumblesnook's wandering theatricals didn't take up *that* much room when you consider the house could accommodate a whole host of homeless monks remember – it's just that she was one of nature's worriers. And when she worried she was in the habit of stuffing even more things into her mouth. *Anything.* Which was why she now had a mouth full of dried pine cones she'd removed from a small dish on the mantelpiece, when Dawkins entered the breakfast room once more. (What happened to the buttons and cleaning crystals in the meantime, I've no idea.)

Dawkins addressed himself to Eddie's Aunt Hetty. 'I have the pony and trap ready, ma'am and will be riding into town to ask Dr Moot to attend Mr Grout at his earliest convenience,' he said.

'Thank you, Dawkins,' said Hetty. 'Please do stress the urgency of my husband's health. I fear for him most dreadfully.'

Dawkins bowed and left.

'Who the devil was that?' asked Mad Uncle Jack.

'Dawkins,' said Mrs Dickens.

'Daphne,' said Mr Dickens.

Eddie sighed and looked at the pattern running around the rim of his empty breakfast plate.

Episode 6

Making a Splash

*In which a doctor pays two visits
and later pays the price*

It transpired – which is a posh word for 'turned out' – that the Dr Moot who came to attend poor Alfie Grout and his terrible cough was *indeed* the same Dr Moot who'd challenged Mad Uncle Jack to a duel all those years before and had shot him twice, but on the one occasion. On the surface, there appeared to be no hard feelings between the two men, though it was obvious in a moment that, to use old-fashioned parlance, he still held a torch for EMAM despite her change of circumstance and the passing years (or, to put it in slightly more modern English: he still fancied

Maud something rotten, despite her being married and having aged like a prune).

There was nothing he'd like more than to sit with Even Madder Aunt Maud in a secluded spot in the garden, holding her tiny hand in his and reading her poems about larks and dewy leaves and sublimely beautiful sunsets tinged with pink. (I know this for a fact because I was given exclusive access to his diary written at the time.) But, in much the same way that the detective inspector, who more often than not turns up in these books, was a good policeman, Dr Moot was a good doctor. At that precise moment, his interests lay first and foremost with his new patient, Alfie Grout, who was married to the niece of the lovely Mad Maud MacMuckle.

It didn't take Dr Moot long to realise what was wrong with Alfie. As a gypsy, he'd never had access to conventional medicine and, as I've explained elsewhere, the particular band of gypsies he was part of, did not include a healer familiar with the old ways and folklore of nature's medicine. Instead, he'd had to make do with chewing lucky heather and that, no pun intended, was the root of the problem. He was full of the stuff. He was a giant version of one of those little pillows stuffed with sweet-smelling lavender that you give your grandmother for Christmas, and she puts it away in a drawer to give to someone else the following year.

'To use a purely non-medical term, Mrs Grout,' said Dr Moot in muted tones, in the corner of the bedroom out of Alfie's earshot, 'he is packed to the gills with the stuff. Once he's free from the heather, I'm sure you'll find him improved beyond recognition.'

'I'll have him stop eating it at once,' said Hetty. 'How long before it – er – passes through the system?'

Dr Moot, who had no humorous characteristics in appearance or character (except for a remarkably droopy moustache and the extraordinary matter of his being besotted by Even Madder Aunt Maud), flipped open his bag and produced a small dark-brown bottle of pills with a handwritten label gummed to one side. 'Give him one of these every morning at the same time,' he instructed. 'No more than one, and it must be swallowed without food or drink.'

'Thank you, doctor,' she said. It was such a relief that Alfie was going to be fine, and to speak to a sane adult once in a while.

There was a problem, though. It lay with the 'swallowed without food or drink' part. Swallowing the pills without food wasn't a problem because one of the last things Uncle Alfie felt like doing in his current condition – hacking cough and being full of not-so-lucky heather – was eating. What he felt like doing was pretty much what he *was* doing, which was being propped up in bed groaning (and he did it very well). The problem was not being allowed to wash down the pills with a drink; not even a glass of water.

The pills weren't enormous. They certainly weren't nearly as large as the ones the vet had insisted on giving Edgar, the horse Eddie had 'acquired' from Mr and Mrs Cruel-Streak when he'd hitched him up to the cow-shaped carnival float – yup, we're talking Marjorie – jam-packed full of children escaping from St Horrid's Home for Grateful Orphans. Edgar had needed the pills when he was being weaned off the diet of rich food the Cruel-Streaks had fed him – which included cheese and biscuits at the end of every meal, washed down with some fine vintage port – and put back onto more ordinary horse fare, of the bag-of-oats variety. These pills had been impressively large. Once, after a particularly fretful game of bridge – not the card game, but a party game of the Dickenses' own invention which involved two teams trying to build a structure long enough and strong enough to support two 'team' members (one on the shoulders of the other) running across the lake at Awful End – Eddie's mother (*aka* Mrs Dickens, *aka* Florinda) had somehow found one of Edgar's horse pills, and had stuffed it in her mouth for comfort. She had no intention of swallowing it and probably couldn't have even if she'd tried. But she did suck it, and suffered the consequences of its medicinal effects.

No one is absolutely clear what followed, least of all Mrs Dickens herself. It was Dawkins who discovered her the following morning in the orangery*, dressed in nothing but a pair of frilly drawers and a bearskin rug, brandishing a poker in one hand and an out-of-date copy of *Bradshaw's* railway timetable in the other. The rather startled gentleman's gentleman later told Ex-Private Gorey – this was before he died, of course, there'd have been little point in talking to him otherwise – that the lady had been screaming at the top of her voice that someone should hurry up and invent the telephone (which, of course, someone already had).

---

* An orangery is like a lemonery, but for oranges.

Whoa! That illustration came as a bit of a surprise, didn't it? I mean, you'd have thought it would have gone somewhere on the previous page next to the part where I first mentioned Eddie's mother in frilly drawers and bearskin rug . . . but, no, just when you are lulled into thinking that such a vivid scene will be left to your own imaginations, you turn the page and: POW, this massive image hits you fair and square – well fair and *oblong*, actually, which is a friendlier word for a rectangle – right between the eyes.

As well as being an *Eddie Dickens* first – it being the first time we've had a full-page David Roberts drawing in the middle of the text – it also gives us an opportunity to take in more of the scene. If you look closely at the bearskin rug, for example, you'll see that it's not – I repeat NOT – the same bearskin rug as the one Mad Uncle Jack collapsed next to on his study floor when he was pronged in the bottom with a toasting fork that time by Even Madder Aunt Maud. It has a very different expression on its face.

Then there's the strange carving on that rather nice stand by the big potted fern. That's one of Eddie's father's sculptures. Research suggests that it depicts 'Jason with the Golden Fleece from Classical Mythology' though, to me, it looks more like 'Tree Man with a Clump of Moss from the Car Boot Sale'.

You'll also have noticed – and, if not, you'll now have to flip back a page to have a look – that there's a pane of broken glass in the orangery. This was probably caused by Mad Uncle Jack's beakiest of beaky noses on the occasion (not previously recounted) when he wanted to prove that he knew every inch of his own home so well that he could walk around it equally well in the dark as in daylight. That was the same occasion that he broke his foot, a pile of 'best' china, and fell out of an upstairs window. This occurred in the days before Eddie and his parents lived at Awful End, so Jack had had to be aided by the then Bishop of Durham, the dinner guest to whom he had made the original (ridiculous) claim.

This only leaves one or two more items of interest to point out in the splendid illustration, before returning to the main action of this final Further Adventure. Firstly, there's the floor which, at first glance, appears to be made of traditional black and white floor tiles, laid out in the traditional checked pattern. Look again, and you'll see that although the white tiles are indeed white tiles, the black 'tiles' are, in truth, very large slices of dried pressed meat.

These had been intended as supplies for an expedition Mad Uncle Jack had been planning to lead in an attempt to discover the Northwest

Passage, whether or not it had been discovered already. Not the northwest passage at Awful End (which led from the boot room to the tack room, or from the tack room to the boot room, depending upon which direction you were going) but the fabled Northwest Passage, a possible route between Europe and the Orient which would make sailing times so much shorter.

Mad Uncle Jack had given up on the expedition when he remembered that he didn't like cold places. The crew he'd assembled got on so well together (without MUJ) that, when the expedition was abandoned, rather than disbanding, they remained friends and opened a seafood restaurant with a nautical theme that became so successful that they opened another one and then another one. Today, there's a whole chain of these restaurants. (You can read about them in an out-of-print paperback entitled *Recipe For Success*.) Never one to waste perfectly good dried pressed meat, Mad Uncle Jack had had the black tiles of the orangery floor pulled up, and the meat trimmed to fit and laid in their place. As to what he did with the black tiles, everyone forgot.

And finally? See that little picture in the oval frame, next to the stuffed heron in the domed glass case? Even Madder Aunt Maud drew that when she was a little girl in Scotland. It's of a butterfly drinking a tankard of foaming ale.

'I can't swallow the pill without water,' said Uncle Alfie, between splutters, the first time he tried.

Aunt Hetty urged him to try again, but it was no good. 'Try chewing it,' she suggested. That was no good either. It was rock hard, and his teeth weren't in the best of condition. 'I'll see if I can grind it into a powder,' she said. 'I'll be back soon, darling.'

Aunt Hetty hurried downstairs into the kitchen and looked for the pestle and mortar. She found the mortar – the bowl part – soon enough, but the pestle – the mini-club part – was nowhere to be seen, which was hardly surprising. Even Madder Aunt Maud had drawn a fish face on it and thrown it into the little formal ornamental pond in the rose garden, for Annabelle to play with.

Rummaging in a drawer by the sink, Aunt Hetty found a steakbeater: an enormous square-headed wooden hammer with some nasty spikes on its head, designed for tenderising meat.

Eddie's Aunt Hetty placed the pill on a cutting block on the kitchen table, raised the steakbeater and brought it down with a resounding crash. The pill didn't break, but the huge wooden hammer did, its head flying loose and hitting –

Now, I must pause here because I want you to

appreciate the problems of being an author. Someone is about to get hit by the head of the steakbeater.

In previous books, in this self-same kitchen, we've had a stray diamond ring (used to grade the size of broad beans) hit Malcolm and subsequently swallowed, in error, by Even Madder Aunt Maud. We've had a piece of devilled kidney fly through the air which, once again deflected by Malcolm, became lodged in the brim of the stovepipe hat of that fairly-well-known engineer, Fandango Jones.

Elsewhere, we've had Eddie's father, Mr Dickens, hit by a falling chimney, fall from a tree (following an explosion), *and* fall from a scaffolding rig onto Dawkins, plus Eddie himself falling from a horse and trap into a gorse bush . . .

. . . and here we go again. Accidents aren't unusual around the place, and yet another one might be seen as 'old hat'. But don't blame the messenger. Another accident there was, and I'm here to tell it like it is.

The flying chunk of wood hit none other than Dr Moot who'd returned to the house that following morning on the pretext of seeing his patient, Alfie Grout, but amongst other things, really in the hope of seeing his beloved Maud again. Instead, he saw stars, or blue birds tweeting around his head, or whatever it is one sees on being knocked unconscious. There was a lot of blood.

Mad Uncle Jack was one of the first on the scene. He'd woken up in his treehouse, washed and shaved at the foot of the ladder with the aid of a mirror – one shard to look into and one particularly sharp piece to use as a razor – and had wandered through the back door in search of a piece of string. Instead, he was confronted by a bloodied Dr Moot lying next to a sack of potatoes.

'Shot him did you?' he asked Hetty. 'Not on my account, I hope? Let bygones be bygones, I always say.'

Aunt Hetty was dumbfounded. Speechless and still brandishing the wooden handle of the steakbeater, she stared down at her unintended victim, shaking in shock at what she'd done.

'Suppose we'd better dispose of the body before that confounded Chief Inspector Bunyon comes sniffing about the place,' said MUJ, matter of factly. Hetty wasn't sure whether her uncle was joking or not. (Bunyon was the detective inspector I referred to a while back. He'd been recently promoted.)

MUJ took charge. He bent down and took Dr Moot's pulse. 'Still alive, I'm afraid,' he said. 'Assuming, that is, that you wanted him dead.'

'I – I –' Hetty spluttered. Mad Uncle Jack already had his hands under the doctor's arms and was dragging him out of the room. Hetty feared that he might be about to bury him or something. She dashed out of the back door after him.

As Mad Uncle Jack dragged the unconscious Moot across a brick courtyard, Eddie appeared around the corner, hands in pockets, humming to himself. He stopped in his tracks. Eddie thought nothing Mad Uncle Jack did could surprise him any more. Here was a man who lived up a tree and paid for everything with dried fish . . . yet, here he now was heaving the blood covered body of Moo-Cow Moot out of the kitchen: Moo-Cow Moot who'd once shot Jack twice (but on the one occasion) and who'd obviously still been in love with his wife.

Did Eddie think, even for a fleeting moment,

71

that MUJ had murdered his rival? We have no way of knowing for sure. What we *can* be sure of, though, is that Eddie wondered what on Earth was going on.

'Tap!' MUJ shouted over to him.

'Tap?' asked Eddie.

'Tap!' MUJ repeated, making the conversation sound like one involving Detective Chief Inspector Bunyon, who was the past master at repeating what the previous person had just said. Mad Uncle Jack jerked his head in the direction of an outside tap – that's a faucet, my American chums – set into a wall.

Eddie ran over and switched it on. There was a spluttering belch followed by an icy jet of water cascading to the ground. With one final heave, his great-uncle unceremoniously dumped Dr Moot in its path. The water had its desired effect. Dr Moot spluttered almost as much as the tap and sat up. The blood momentarily washed from the wound on his forehead, Eddie could make out a strange pattern on his skin. It was almost as if someone had hit him with a steakb-e-a-t-e-r . . .

Eddie gasped. What was that *thing* mild-mannered Aunt Hetty was holding in her hand?

Remembrance of Things Past

In which readers are given a short account of the death of Malcontent, and meet a very short man

Once upon a time, not *that* long ago, there lived a man named Squire Dickens and he owned all the land as far as the eye could see (and he had very good eyesight). The squire had a number of children, but his son-and-heir was Malcontent Dickens, whom the less cloth-eared of you may remember my having mentioned before. The first thing Malcontent did on inheriting Awful End when his father died, was to have it pulled down, and the Awful End that Eddie knew built in its place.

Today, it's one of the finest examples of a Victorian manor house in Britain, in either private or public hands. The only slight shame is that some of the building materials Malcontent used were substandard to say the least: downright shoddy would be more accurate, which is why parts of it were crumbling just a few years after Malcontent's death (and partly to blame for the chimney landing on Eddie's father that time). Such materials included bits of the old house, bits found lying around, and even bits stolen from nearby walls and other houses. The story goes that the vicarage over at Stourgate disappeared overnight, with the vicar and his favourite cat, Hook, still in it.

Possibly the finest room in the entire house was the private chapel, with richly-carved woodwork throughout. Malcontent was not a particularly religious man but, just to be on the safe side, prayed seven or eight times a day, and more on Sundays, and had an effigy of God on a cloud in his bedroom. The woodwork in the chapel and the effigy in the bedroom were carved by a master-craftsman by the name of Geo Gibbons. I assume that Geo was shot for George – very short, in fact – but this hardly matters because, ever since he first picked up an awl – which may sound like a sea-bird but is, apparently, some form of woodworking tool – he was known as Grinning Gibbons. Why? Because carving wood made him grin like an idiot. Here's a diagram to prove it:

Fig 1.
Grinning
Gibbons

Fig 2.
Grinning
Idiot

Hmmm. The idiot that David Roberts drew reminds me of someone . . . Now, where was I? Yes, Malcontent Dickens, son of Squire Dickens. He lived into his fifties but had had every intention of living far longer. Sadly, Fate had had other ideas (which is also why we're left with two 'had had's together in a few short lines). Fate is often spelled with a capital 'F' – and not just at the beginning of sentences – because it's such an important thing. It's Fate which decides whether you're the one who wins the outsized cuddly polar bear in the raffle, or whether it's you or the person next to you who gets soaked in muddy water when the passing buffalo stampede the water hole.

In the case of Dr Malcontent Dickens, Fate decreed that he be walking past Wyndham Field the day that the stalls and tents of the Lamberley Fayre were pitched on it, just as Count Orville The Amazing Human Cannonball was fired from his custom-built cannon . . . and Fate decided that the cannon would inexplicably lurch and tilt down at the point of firing so, instead of his usual trajectory of up-and-over the heads of the cheering crowds, Count Orville (whose real name was Thomas Plunke) flew past the startled onlookers to their right, and ploughed into Eddie's great grandfather. The human cannonball survived, not least because he'd been wearing body armour, including a metal helmet of his own design. Malcontent Dickens didn't, not least because the human cannonball had been wearing body armour, including a metal helmet of his own design.

Malcontent's funeral was an impressive affair. As well as the black horses with plumes on their heads – rather like those pulling the hearse containing the coffin containing the very-much-alive Great Zucchini, in one of Eddie's previous adventures – there were many official mourners who'd never known Dr Malcontent Dickens in life, but were paid to weep and wail and generally moan in sadness at his untimely passing. One such official mourner was Gherkin the dwarf.

Because there weren't funerals everyday and not every funeral required his services anyway, Gherkin was only a part-time mourner. Amongst other things – make a note of that – he was also a part-time freak in a freakshow, a mummer (not to be confused with a mamma), and an occasional tumbler – one who tumbles, not the drinking tumbler variety – in a touring group of undersized acrobats called 'The Remarkably Small Garfields' which wasn't the catchiest of names, even in the 19th century. The pretence was that the troupe was made up of members of the Garfield family who were all, for some unexplained reason, remarkably small. This conceit was wholly unconvincing, not least because some of the 'Garfields' were, like Gherkin, dwarfs whilst others were what they called midgets. Also, all of them were Chinese except for Gherkin and the midget Ebony, who was a black African.

At funerals, Gherkin was by far the best blubberer. He would fight back tears, sob uncontrollably and blow his nose on a white silk handkerchief almost as big as he was. At Malcontent's funeral, Malcontent's widow, Ivy Dickens (*née* Porker) was so impressed by Gherkin's grief that, though she'd already paid extra to have him as a part of her husband's funeral cortège, she pressed a gold sovereign into the hand

of Mr Gagstaff of the funeral directors *Gagstaff, Wagg and Homily* and, between whimpers, asked that it be given to 'the little man'. As it was, Mr Gagstaff put the money on a horse – not literally, he placed a bet – which, to his considerable surprise, won its race. Out of the winnings, he passed half-a-crown to Gherkin which, though not as much as a sovereign, was not to be sniffed at.

Also at the funeral that day were Malcontent and Ivy's three sons, George, Jack (MUJ) and Percy. Jack had been fascinated by Gherkin at the funeral and couldn't take his eyes off him. Whilst he should have been lamenting the untimely

78

passing of his father, he found himself wondering whether he'd be able to lift the dwarf with one hand, or to wear him in a gold cage around his neck. He was wondering where he might be able to buy such a cage, or whether he'd have to have one specially made.

'Excuse me,' said MUJ sidling up beside Gherkin once the door to the Dickens family vault had been closed on his father's coffin. 'Might I have a word with you?'

'Surely, sir,' said Gherkin, looking up at this thinnest of thin young gentlemen.

'I was wondering whether you could fit inside this box?'

The dwarf looked at the empty wooden crate stamped **EAST INDIA COMPANY**, which the beakiest-of-beaky-nosed young men seemed to have pulled out from behind a bush to the side of the mausoleum. He thought it rather an odd thing for a son of the deceased to be dragging around at a funeral. 'I suspect I might be able to, sir,' he said, a little hesitantly, 'should the need arise.'

'Would you mind stepping inside it, just to be sure?'

'I'm afraid that won't be possible at present,' said Gherkin, looking across to Mr Gagstaff, who was deep in conversation with the widow. 'I'm still on duty.'

'I see, I see,' said Jack. 'Perhaps you would be kind enough to call on me at your earliest convenience and to try the box for size then?' He put his hand in his pocket and handed Gherkin something. 'My card,' he said.

Gherkin looked in his palm. He was holding what appeared to be a very small, very dried, fish.

★

Now I expect that one or two of you – if there's more than one person reading this – are thinking, *That's all very well, but why is that nice Mr Ardagh suddenly telling us all of this? What does this have to do with Mad Uncle Jack pouring water on Moo-Cow Moot – with the bloody imprint of a steakbeater on his forehead – whilst being watched by a mortified Aunt Hetty and a flabbergasted Eddie?* Well, you're about to find out. I'm not sure who it was who said 'Patience is a virtue/Virtue is a Grace/And Grace is a little girl/Who wouldn't wash her face' but I do hope:

1. That it's out of copyright; and
2. They'll be quiet and leave me alone . . .

because Fate is about to play a big hand again.

★

Eddie and Mad Uncle Jack helped the groaning Dr Moot to his feet. Blood was still pouring from the poor doctor's head wound and he was now soaked through with cold water from the outside tap.

At least he's alive, thought Eddie, looking across at his Aunt Hetty, who still looked mortified.

Moot lost his footing and staggered to the left, nearly knocking Eddie off his feet. The height difference between Eddie and his extraordinarily thin, tall great-uncle didn't make them an ideal partnership for supporting a semiconscious man under each arm.

'Steady on, boy!' MUJ ordered then, suddenly completely distracted by something or *someone*, he let go of Moot altogether, causing Eddie and the doctor to land, unceremoniously, on the ground in a heap of writhing arms and legs.

The distraction was, indeed, a someone and that someone was an elderly dwarf striding as fast as his little legs would carry him.

Episode 8

Lurkin' with Gherkin

*In which Eddie befriends an extraordinary man
and enjoys a hearty breakfast*

Now, dear reader, *you* know that the man was Gherkin and *I* know that the man was Gherkin and there's absolutely no doubt in my mind that Mad Uncle Jack knew that the man was Gherkin – not least because he gasped, 'Gherkin!' in amazement – but, at this stage of the proceedings, Eddie had never even heard of the man, nor knew of his role in great-grandfather's funeral.

When Eddie heard the word 'Gherkin!' pass MUJ's lips he, quite understandably, assumed that it was an oath – a swear word of sorts – that his great uncle was muttering as a result of an apparent stranger stumbling upon the unfortunate scene of the family trying to revive an innocent doctor who had been beaten over the head with a meat tenderiser by one Aunt Hetty. He was even more surprised, therefore, when the elderly dwarf thrust a very grubby dog-eared calling card into Mad Uncle Jack's hand. Eddie could see that it read:

MAD JACK DICKENS, Esq.
Awful End

'I came at my earliest convenience,' said Gherkin, his voice deep. He must have been busy. A great many years had passed since MUJ gave him that card (after that fish) at Malcontent's funeral.

Despite the dwarf probably being the oldest person present and, undoubtedly, the smallest, he was also immensely strong – and not just for his size. Having assessed the situation, and waiting for neither instruction nor invitation, he hoisted the dazed Dr Moot up onto his back, in a position known today as 'the fireman's lift', and carried him back into the house, jogging across the brick courtyard with a bouncing gait that even the butcher's young delivery boy couldn't achieve with a far lesser weight of meat on his shoulders.

Before anyone else knew quite what was going on, Gherkin had positioned Dr Moot in a semi-upright position on a Knowle sofa, and rustled him up two fingers of Irish whiskey in a crystal-cut glass. Moments later, he was applying a linen napkin to the doctor's wound. He then lifted the doctor's own hand to it. 'If you'd be good enough to hold this here, sir,' he said.

The befuddled doctor nodded appreciatively. He felt in safe hands. They *all* felt in safe hands. For the first time since the head of the steakbeater had come flying off and hit Dr Moot, Aunt Hetty felt that things might turn out right after all. Eddie also felt that, despite their saviour's unusual appearance (as in looks) and unexplained appearance (as in arrival-on-the-scene), an air of authority and *sanity* had descended on the proceedings.

Mad Uncle Jack, who'd had the initiative to revive old Moo-Cow Moot by sticking his head under the tap, was simply rather pleased that the little fellow from his father's funeral had been true to his word and shown up, even if a little later than he'd hoped.

It was soon after Dr Moot had found himself able to speak, and to accept Aunt Hetty's profound apologies for what had happened – particularly when it transpired that she'd been trying to crush one of the pills that he'd supplied for her husband, Alfie – that Dawkins entered the room. He was horrified to see Dr Moot drinking whiskey. It was *his* job to hand out drinkies as and when required. It would be bad enough if Mad Mister Dickens (MUJ) or Mr Dickens (Eddie's father) or Mr Grout (Uncle Alfie) started pouring their own drinks, and unheard of for the ladies to do so, but for a complete stranger to come into the house and pour out a whiskey for another – a mighty small, complete stranger, at that – well, it was unheard of! An outrage! It was *his* job and no-one else's. It wasn't that Dawkins actually liked pouring their drinks, far from it, in fact. Many was the occasion, in truth, when he'd thought, *'Why don't they pour their own stupid drinks? They're not babies!'* but, at this precise moment, that wasn't the point.

How did he know that it was the dwarf who'd poured the drink? Because none of the others would have. That's how.

Dawkins cleared his throat and was about to try to convey how hurt he felt (without overstepping the mark in the servant/master relationship, of course) when he felt something sinking its teeth into his bottom. He spun around with a yelp, to come face to face not with the young crocodile, as expected, but Even Madder Aunt Maud. She was smirking.

'I don't see why Annabelle should have all the fun,' she said, scrambling to her feet, Malcolm tucked under one arm.

'Indeed not, madam,' said Dawkins, all thoughts of whiskey now forgotten.

'Ah, there you are, er –'

'Dawkins, sir.'

'Dawkins,' said Mad Uncle Jack. 'Would you be good enough to lay an extra place for breakfast and then take Dr Moot home in his horse and trap? I don't want him bleeding all over the place here.'

'Very good, sir,' said Dawkins.

'Don't you think he should at least stay here until he's –' began Hetty.

'Nonsense! Nonsense!' said MUJ, with a dismissive wave of one of his thinnest of thin arms.

'Shouldn't he at least see a doctor?' Hetty protested.

'Perhaps he could look in a mirror!' snorted Even Madder Aunt Maud.

'I shall be fine, Mrs Grout,' Dr Moot assured her. 'Please think nothing of it. Accidents do happen.' His voice sounded rather weak and wobbly.

'Good, that's settled then,' said Mad Uncle Jack. 'Get him off my property as soon as possible, er –'

'Dawkins, sir,' said Dawkins.

'Yes,' said Mad Uncle Jack. 'Exactly.'

Gherkin strode over to the gentleman's gentleman, went up on tiptoe, and whispered something in his ear. Dawkins nodded.

Eddie realised what the whispering must have been about when he was the first to enter the breakfast room for – you guessed it, the clue being in the name and all – breakfast.

Not only had an extra place been laid at the table but the chair at that place had a footstool next to it and a pile of books* on it, topped by a comfy cushion. When Gherkin came into the room some five minutes or so after Eddie (who was tucking into a pile of bacon) he stepped up onto the footstool and positioned himself on the chair.

* These were a selection of books about Australia, which played a small but vital part in the second of these Further Adventures, *Horrendous Habits*. The books that is, not Australia.

'My name is Gherkin,' he said.

'I'm Edmund – Eddie – Dickens,' said Eddie. 'My parents and I moved here when our own home was destroyed by fire. Mad Uncle – Mad *Mister* Dickens is my great-uncle.'

'I see,' said Gherkin. 'It is very good of your great-uncle to receive me in this manner.'

'I'm not sure I understand, sir,' said Eddie.

'I am not a gentleman,' the dwarf explained. 'I was a humble showman and a professional mourner, retired now, of course.'

'Mourner?' asked Eddie.

By way of an answer, Gherkin burst into (very convincing) tears and picked up a napkin, using it like a hanky to dab his eyes. A moment later, he stopped, as though nothing had happened. 'At funerals,' he said.

'Aha!' said Eddie, clearly fascinated.

'It was at a funeral that I met your great-uncle on the one and only occasion until now.'

'Really?' said Eddie.

'Really,' nodded Gherkin. 'He took an instant interest in me. Some people find it awkward to discuss my height with me, as though being small might somehow be embarrassing, but not him.'

Eddie took another mouthful of bacon.

'He wanted to know whether I was able to fit in a box of a particular size, and, having presented me

88

with his card, seemed to be entertaining the idea of wearing me in a cage around his neck.'

'You're not that small!' Eddie blurted, instantly hoping that he hadn't overstepped the mark.

'No,' said Gherkin. 'I'm not. Your great-uncle would need extremely strong neck muscles to achieve such a feat.'

'Whose funeral was it, if you don't mind my asking?' said Eddie.

The dwarf thought for a moment. 'If Mad Mr Jack Dickens is your great-uncle, then the deceased must have been your great-grandfather.'

'Dr Malcontent Dickens?' said Eddie in surprise, 'Then you can't have seen Mad Uncle Jack in a very long time indeed!'

'Indeed,' agreed Gherkin. He eyed Eddie's plate.

'You have to help yourself at breakfast,' Eddie explained, nodding in the direction of the silver-domed warmers laid out on the side table keeping the various dishes hot.

'Thank you,' said Gherkin. 'I'm not really used to the ways of life in such a grand house.' He was about to climb down via the footstool, when Fabian came into the room (wearing a pair of slippers that Eddie's mother, Mrs Dickens, had given Eddie the previous Christmas). Gherkin looked from Fabian to Eddie and then back again. 'Twins?' he asked.

'Cousins,' said Eddie. 'This is Mister Gherkin. Mr Gherkin, this is Fabian.'

'Ah,' nodded the dwarf. 'The son of the poor lady who inadvertently injured the doctor.'

Fabian's eyes narrowed. 'Haven't we met before, Mr Gherkin?' he asked.

'It's possible, I suppose,' said Gherkin, 'but, in all honesty, I don't recall, Master Fabian. And, please, it's not *Mister* Gherkin, just plain Gherkin.'

'Isn't it your real name, then?' asked Fabian. He was already at the side table shovelling scrambled eggs onto a plate.

'I never knew my real name if I had one, nor my parents,' explained Gherkin. 'According to the very long and badly-spelled note that was written on a luggage label and tied around my neck when I was left outside Bramworth's Stern But Fair Home For Foundlings, my mother – whoever she was – had wanted to keep me, but my father – whoever he was – had taken one look at me and decided not to.'

'How awful!' said Eddie.

'Kind of you to say so, Master Edmund,' said the dwarf, 'but at least my mother left me on the steps of the foundlings' home. Many babies suffer far worse.'

Eddie was about to tell Gherkin about the St Horrid's Home for Grateful Orphans escapees . . .

when Even Madder Aunt Maud entered the breakfast room.

She took one look at Gherkin teetering on the top of his pile of books and gave one of her most indignant-sounding indignant snorts. 'Ridiculous!' she said. 'A grown man trying to read so many books at once, and with his *bottom*!'

Episode 9

Warts and All

In which a famous painter arrives at
Awful End and probably wishes that he hadn't

No one was thrilled at the prospect of the arrival of A. C. Pryden, to paint the official portrait of Mad Major Jack Dickens for the War Office. Under normal circumstances, Mr Dickens might have been delighted at the prospect of the arrival of a 'fellow artist' . . . but he was currently going through his play-writing phase, and felt MUJ having his picture painted was an intrusion. The performance of his as-yet untitled play in the grounds of Awful End was supposed to be the highlight of the Dickenses' artistic calendar for that year and he didn't want some world-famous professional portrait painter getting all the attention.

Eddie was more concerned that some serious harm might come to the great painter. If Even Madder Aunt Maud's stuffed stoat didn't get him, perhaps her baby croc would? And the crumbling chimney stack falling on his own dear father hadn't happened *that* long ago, though now he was almost fully recovered. (The one lasting side effect was that Mr Dickens could now rotate his head on his neck through almost 360 degrees, in much the same way that an owl can).

For the reputation of the family, Eddie thought it best if *he* was to meet Mr Pryden (who had insisted on travelling by train). Excusing himself from that morning's rehearsal (in which Mr Pumblesnook was playing just about everyone except for the bush over which the character of Mad Aunt Maud first lays eyes on Fabian's wheel-on version of Marjorie the hollow cow), he arrived at the railway station a matter of minutes before the train pulled into the platform.

Eddie was standing by the pony and trap just outside when the great painter emerged, handing his pasteboard ticket to a smartly dressed ticket collector, brass buttons glinting in the sun.

Following Pryden was a railway porter, wheeling Pryden's luggage (including a large artist's easel) on a trolley similar to the one that Eddie's father, Mr Dickens, had once been lashed to when he needed to get around with his bad back.

'Mr Pryden?' asked Eddie politely.

'Yes,' said A. C. Pryden with a curt nod. Much has been written about Pryden's paintings (and you'll find reproductions of his pictures in most books on 19th-century portraiture), but some have also written about his voice.

The general consensus is that he spoke like a penguin would speak if penguins could speak. Apparently, it had an extraordinary quality to it. You could hear the penguin waddle in it. You could imagine his words being spoken by a beak rather than a mouth. Here he was, a man and a very successful one at that, sounding as if he was rather hoping that he could go diving off ice-floes.

'I'm Eddie Dickens. Edmund. Major Jack Dickens is my great-uncle, and I'm to take you to Awful End.'

'Very good,' said Pryden.

The railway porter heaved the painter's luggage up into the back of the trap. Pryden fumbled in his pocket and produced a tartan purse with a large clasp. He undid the clasp and took out a silver thrupenny bit which he handed to the man.

'Thank you kindly, sir,' said the porter, putting his finger to the peak of his cap in the manner of a form of salute. He whistled as he wheeled the empty trolley back towards the station entrance.

Pryden climbed up onto the slatted board seat on one side, then Eddie climbed up the other side and sat next to him, taking the reins in his hand.

The journey was uneventful. A local greengrocer shouted abuse on recognising the horse, having been in dispute with MUJ for many years over the matter of his squeezing the fruit but never buying any; the ironmonger ran alongside the trap at one stage, long enough to thrust a parcel of dried fish (addressed to Eddie's father) into his hand – fish with which MUJ had paid for various items in the recent past, for which Mr Dickens would substitute real money by return of post – and a few members of the local hunt (some still in bandages) raised a fist as Eddie and his passenger passed *The Pickled Trout* (a local ale house). A. C. Pryden looked more puzzled than put out, and was too polite to say anything.

The ride up the gravel drive was a long one and, every once in a while, through gaps in the foliage, or across the lawn, Pryden would catch a glimpse of children beating each other with what appeared to be cucumbers.

'They're actors,' Eddie explained hurriedly. 'They're rehearsing the role of orphans escaping from a truly horrible orphanage.'

'I see,' said Pryden. What Eddie didn't add was that – as both you know and I know – most of the actors playing the escaping orphans really were escaped orphans. He wasn't sure what the law's opinion on the matter would be, or what Mr Pryden's opinion of the law was. 'And what play, pray, is that?'

'It doesn't have a title as yet,' Eddie explained. 'My father wrote it.'

'Most interesting,' said the painter, in just the way that a penguin would, no doubt, have said 'most interesting' if penguins could say 'most interesting'.

For those of you who find such details add flavour, I should say that the 'cucumbers' were, in reality, another fine example of Fabian's recently discovered prop-making skills. They were made from painted rolled-up newspaper. As for why the children were hitting each other when, during their actual escape they were hitting – or intending to hit

– their captors, this was down to youthful exuberance and the fact that Mr and Mrs Pumblesnook were off somewhere doing whatever it was she did with the blotches she peeled from her visage (*aka* her face). Whilst their backs were turned, the young actors and actresses were letting off steam.

Mrs Dickens was standing at the entrance to the house, there to greet the well-known painter on his arrival. 'Welcome to Awful End,' she said. What A. C. Pryden heard was '*Weowm oo Awwel En*' because Eddie's mother had stuffed her mouth with gravel from the drive, pieces of which were now falling from her lips. At that moment, Dawkins, Mr Dickens's gentleman's gentleman, arrived with a silver salver, in the middle of which rested a schooner of sherry.

'Some refreshment after your long journey, sir?' he asked, proffering Pryden the drink.

'Thank you,' said Even Madder Aunt Maud, snatching the glass as she appeared around the corner. She downed the sherry in one, then tossed the empty glass over her shoulder. Eddie could have sworn he'd heard a muffled 'Ouch'.

A. C. Pryden may well have wished that he could have clambered back onto the trap and caught the next train out of there, but the commission was an important one. If the War

97

Office wanted him to paint a war hero, then a war hero he would paint . . . at least he thought he would. He had no idea of Mad Uncle Jack's appalling military record.

Two of MUJ's ex-privates helped unload Pryden's luggage, carrying most of it to the room which had been set aside as his studio. The rest was taken to his bedroom (except for one small case which never made it to either, and was found years later with the single addition of a mummified mouse which, in its pre-mummified state, had somehow found its way inside it but, sadly, not its way out again). Eddie's mother hurried off to the kitchen to prepare lunch.

'I should like to see my subject as soon as possible,' Mr Pryden told Eddie, 'even if only to watch him from afar . . . to get the measure of the man.'

'Subject?' snorted Even Madder Aunt Maud, who was now leading Annabelle on her silver chain up the porch steps. The baby crocodile had short legs so more slithered forward on her belly than climbed each individual step. 'You're not a king are you?'

'Mr Pryden means the subject of his painting, Mad Aunt Maud,' Eddie quickly explained. 'Not a royal subject.'

'Aha! My beloved Jack, you mean?' she asked, stopping in the open doorway.

98

'If you are the wife of Major Jack Dickens, madam, then yes,' said the painter. Then, after a pause, he added. 'Is that a – er – crocodile?'

Even Madder Aunt Maud looked at Malcolm, tucked neatly under one arm. 'Don't be so utterly ridiculous!' she exclaimed. 'He's a stoat. A stuffed stoat! Call yourself a painter, and you can't even tell a mammal from a reptile.'

'He was referring to Annabelle, EMAM!' said Eddie, who was still at an age when he felt he had to compensate for his relatives if not actually apologise for them. Annabelle was busy pulling on her silver lead. She wanted to get inside the house.

'Oh *her*,' said his great-aunt. 'Yes, Mr Pringle, she is most definitely a crocodile. How observant.'

'Pryden.'

'I beg your pardon?'

'Pryden.'

'Pardon me?'

'You said Pringle.'

'I said pardon,' frowned Even Madder Aunt Maud.

'Prior to pardon you said Pringle.'

'What of it, Mr Pringle?'

'My name is Pryden.'

'Mine is Maud. Maud Dickens, Mr Pryden Pringle.'

Anyone who knew Even Madder Aunt Maud

would have given up at this stage. Sadly, A. C. Pryden did not (know her, nor give up).

'Mrs Dickens, it is plain Pryden!' he said, as emphatically as someone who sounded like a penguin could be emphatic.

'Plain Pryden Pringle? Is there a hyphen in there, somewhere, sir? And why do you want to measure my husband? If his height's so important, can't you simply draw around him?'

At that precise moment, Dawkins reappeared wearing a striped apron and brandishing a dustpan and brush. He began sweeping up the tiny shards of broken sherry glass in the hall.

Eddie seized the opportunity to grab the grateful Mr Pryden by the hand and through the front door into the house.

'Let me show you to your room, sir,' he said.

'Th-thank you,' said the great portrait painter, still recovering from the shock of his first encounter with Even Madder Aunt Maud.

Most (normal) people who met EMAM went through a variety of different overlapping stages. Stage One was Confusion. Believing themselves to be speaking to someone quite sane, they would try to understand what was being said and wondered whether it was *they*, not her, who wasn't making sense. Stage Two was Realisation. This was the stage when people began to realise that Even

Madder Aunt Maud didn't have all her marbles/was more than one sandwich short of a picnic/that the lights may be on but that there was no-one at home/that she was battier than a belfry . . . and so on and so on. Stage Three was Exasperation. This was the period when people thought, somewhat foolishly in my opinion, that if only they spoke firmly enough and clearly enough, they might somehow 'get through' to Even Madder Aunt Maud and make her see sense. (I feel that this might be better known as the 'Pull The Other One' Stage or even the 'You've Got To Be Kidding' Stage.) Stage Four was Denial: this can't really be happening to me. Surely no-one's really as crazy as this old bat seems to be?!?

Of course, not everyone went through all these different stages when dealing with EMAM, nor necessarily in the same order, but that was certainly the common pattern and, nine times out of ten, the final stage – Stage Five, in this instance – was Attempted Flight. In other words, trying to put as much distance between themselves and Even Madder Aunt Maud as possible.

I've no doubt that, despite his excellent upbringing, A. C. Pryden would have found a way of separating himself from EMAM sooner or later, but the fact that Master Eddie Dickens had rescued him, gave him a respect and liking for the boy; a respect which was to grow as he found out just how bonkers the rest of the Dickens family were, even the very subject of his painting, Major Jack Dickens.

A. C. Pryden and MUJ met for the first time that evening. Somewhat unusually, Mad Uncle Jack was brandishing a home-made spear, or harpoon, made from a two-tined (pronged) carving fork bound to the end of a broom handle. He wore no clothes except for a loin cloth made from old copies of *The Times* newspaper, and had smeared his face, arms and torso with lines of soot.

'Good evening, Major,' said Pryden, leaping up from his chair and extending his hand in greeting. 'It is a pleasure to meet you.' He hoped that he hadn't looked too startled when he'd first caught sight of Jack Dickens walking through the door. 'Are you fresh from rehearsals?'

'Rehearsals?'

'The play. Your great-nephew Edmund informed me that his father had written a play and –'

'What on Earth gave you the idea that I might be a party to such theatricals?' Mad Uncle Jack demanded.

Silent alarm bells rang in Pryden's mind. It had suddenly dawned on him that Major Dickens was probably as barmy as his good lady wife but, despite this, he thought he should explain. 'Your costume, sir. Your –'

'Costume? What costume?' asked a genuinely confused MUJ.

Oh, Lord! thought the painter. What if he dresses like this all the time? He cleared his throat, making a sound not at all dissimilar to how a penguin might sound clearing *his* throat. 'I was referring to the – er – body painting and the – er – home-made spear, Major,' he explained. 'It's not often one sees someone dressed in such a manner. A once in a lifetime experience, I should say.' He smiled weakly (which doesn't mean once every seven days, but in a weak fashion).

At that precise moment, as if on cue, a very small man entered the room. He was brandishing a home-made spear, or harpoon, made from a two-tined (pronged) carving fork bound to the end of a broom handle. He wore no clothes except for a loin cloth made from old copies of *The Times* newspaper, and had smeared his face, arms and torso with lines of soot. It was Gherkin. Polite or not, A. C. Pryden, FRA*, sat back down again, gripping the arms of his chair.

---

* FRA means Fellow of the Royal Academy, though some painters unlucky enough to achieve such an honour have claimed that it actually stands for Frightfully Rotten Artist.

'Aha!' said Mad Uncle Jack. 'See what you mean. Should explain. This fine chap here –' He slapped the dwarf on the back '– is Gherkin. Want him in the picture with me.'

'Is he a Pygmy?' asked Pryden politely, having read about tribes of small people. 'Is this his – er – traditional dress?'

'No, Mr Pryden,' Gherkin replied, perfectly able to speak for himself. 'I am, first and foremost, an Englishman.'

'And a dwarf,' MUJ added.

'Apologies,' said Pryden. 'And you want him in

the – er – painting with you, you say, Major?'

'I thought it might liven things up a little. I imagine that the walls of the War Office are lined with row after row of portraits of chaps in uniform, so why not wear something different?'

'And what exactly are you dressed *as*, if you don't mind my asking?'

'An abory-jine,' said MUJ. 'Saw a picture of one in a book sent over from Australia. They're the native people. Apparently the place is crawling with them –'

'Ah. An aborigine!' nodded Pryden, trying to find the words to tell Major Dickens what he'd have to tell him next.

'That's the fellow. I should add that, believe it or not, these aren't actually authentic aborigine clothing or weapons.' He pointed to his newspaper loin cloth and broom-handle-and-carving-fork spear. 'But close approximations, made by our own fair hands.'

'Precisely,' said Gherkin. 'We don't for one minute believe a genuine aborigine would wear *The Times*.'

'Probably can't get it over there,' nodded MUJ. 'Must use the Australian equivalent.'

A. C. Pryden wanted to cry.

Intermission

There now follows a brief intermission*

Hello, again. How embarrassing. I was about to make myself a cup of tea in this strange kitchen, when it suddenly occurred to me that some of you may have been wondering whatever happened to Harry and Thunk.

* PLEASE NOTE: This picture of the author dressed as a chicken bears no relation to the text. Because this is an unauthorised intermission – neither sanctioned by the publishers, nor appearing in the index – no money has been allocated for an accompanying illustration. It was half-inched** by the author from *Horrendous Habits*, when somebody's back was turned.

** Half-inched = pinched = stolen

There they were right at the start of things, so early on in the book, in fact, that the page they're on isn't even numbered – it was the piece entitled 'Prologue', if you skipped it – and we haven't had so much as a peep out of them since.

Well, I can soon put that right. (I'm the author, which in Eddie's world is a bit like being a god, only the hours are shorter and you still have to worry about a pension for your old age.)

Before I do that, and before anyone decides to write and ask me about it, I should explain what I mean by 'strange kitchen'. Firstly, it is simply strange as in *unfamiliar* because this isn't my house and I don't know where everything is. Preparing every beverage, snack, or meal is a learning curve. Secondly, it's strange as in *peculiar* because if you lift one of the work surfaces it reveals a bath. *The* bath. And I just can't get my head around the idea of bathing in the kitchen, whether my wife is standing next to me peeling sprouts or not.

And so to Messrs. Harry and Thunk.

HARRY: You're late.
THUNK: Sorry, 'arry. I ran into a spot of bother at the *'orse and 'ounds*. Nuffink I couldn't 'andle.
HARRY: I've 'eard from our informant.
THUNK: Our whats, 'arry?

HARRY: Our eyes and ears what was inside the Dickens 'ousehold.

THUNK: Your man inside Awful End?

HARRY: Sssh! Keep your voice down. Yes. That's who I mean. He says that them Dickenses are a bunch of lunatics sittin' on some very valuable items indeed . . . and he's told me the best time to strike.

THUNK: An' will that be soon, 'arry?

HARRY: Real soon, Thunk.

THUNK: So we can stop standing in this ditch?

HARRY: That we can, Thunk.

Now, back to the main action. Enjoy.

Episode 10

State of Play

*In which the portrait is completed
and preparations for the play well under way*

The news which A. C. Pryden hadn't been looking forward to imparting to Mad Uncle Jack was twofold: firstly, that the War Office had insisted he be painted wearing his full dress (posh occasion) uniform and, secondly, that he – and he alone – would appear in the painting. There was no room for anyone else: even someone as small as Gherkin.

When the artist finally got around to telling MUJ, Eddie's great-uncle seemed decidedly unbothered. His mind had moved on to other things. He was puzzled, for example, by his almost uncontrollable urge to throw Mr Pryden one of his dried fish, even expecting him to swallow it whole. 'It was the damnedest thing,' he later commented to Eddie's mother.

Much to everyone's amazement, the actual sittings – when MUJ sat and Pryden sketched or painted – went surprisingly well. Mad Uncle Jack didn't need to be in front of the portrait all the time whilst the artist was painting. Pryden would carry on working on it between sittings, making any tiny alterations and corrections with the stroke of a brush or the scrape of a palette knife at the following sitting. He even grew to rather like the old fellow, but he wouldn't let him see the oil painting before it was completed. No one could. (It rested on his easel, hidden by a curtain.) No one except Eddie, that is.

You will recall that A. C. Pryden believed that he'd found an ally in Eddie – a lifeboat of sanity in a sea of madness – and didn't want to lose him. Eddie's Aunt Hetty seemed pleasant enough, but she had a sick husband to tend to, and seemed racked with guilt about something. As for the rest of them – the mad major and his even madder wife aside – they seemed to be wrapped up in putting on this play of theirs, apart from Eddie's mother who was forever filling her mouth with whatever was to hand, which, on her one and only visit to Pryden's makeshift studio, included little tubes of oil paint. Fortunately, he always carried spares.

Then the day came when, much sooner than most of them had expected, the picture was completed.

'Why don't you unveil it on Monday, before the first-night opening of the play, sir?' Eddie suggested when he heard the news. 'You'll have a ready made audience.'

'Of course, the official unveiling will be at a small ceremony at the War Office itself,' A. C. Pryden reminded him, 'but it would be an excellent opportunity to show it to the Major, his family and friends. A capital idea, Edmund!'

Eddie's father was less than pleased. 'That's supposed to be *my* night, Eddie,' he said. '*Our* night. Mine because I wrote it. Yours because the play is all about your life –'

'Well, a version of it, father –'

'*And* you play the leading role on stage. Having A. C. Pryden unveil his picture of your great-uncle would . . . well, would steal your limelight.' (The especially bright light at the front of stages used to be created by burning lime, which is where the phrase comes from, if you were wondering.)

'It makes perfect sense, father,' said Eddie.

111

'After all, Mad Uncle Jack has been a big part of my life since I first headed for Awful End.'

The orphan girl playing Even Madder Aunt Maud happened to be waddling by at that moment. She hit Eddie over the head with her papier-mâché Malcolm. 'Drink more milk!' she snapped, stomping off. This particular aspect of acting is called 'staying in character.'

'She's very good, isn't she?' said Mr Dickens.

'Very,' agreed Eddie, rubbing the top of his head. If the truth be told, one of Eddie's greatest fears regarding the whole play was how MUJ and EMAM would react. Would they be outraged? It wasn't that his father had written anything particularly outrageous about them, it was just that they were inclined to take offence at the slightest thing . . .

. . . and if they *were* outraged, how would they express it? He wasn't worried about shouts from the audience, or one of them stomping off in disgust, though he'd far rather they loved every minute of it, of course, and showered him with accolades*. No, what bothered him was that they might storm the stage and take matters into their own hands.

* a type of champagne**
** a terrible lie

When Eddie raised the matter with the actor-manager-director-cum-just-about-everything-else, Mr Pumblesnook, he simply chuckled and said, 'The whole *raison d'être* behind acting is to stimulate an emotional response from your audience, me boy! Joy . . . sadness . . . anger . . . rage. All is fuel for the actor's craft!'

'I'm thinking more about actors getting hurt. Being hit with Malcolm is no joke –'

Mr Pumblesnook grinned, to reveal a chipped tooth. 'You're forgetting that I too have been a victim of the stoat's scorn,' he boomed. 'But when in character, a good actor must simply overcome such distractions.'

'But –'

'I remember being horse-whipped by an agent of the Shah of Persia who leapt up onto the stage during *Turban Trysts* in Greenwich back in '56. If anything, it made my performance all the more riveting. As he was dragged from the stage, rest assured that all eyes remained on me. I had that audience under my spell, and it would take more than a few tattered clothes and a few dozen, painful lashes to put me off my stride!' he said. 'It was only a matter of weeks before the welts stopped bleeding and the pain subsided.'

If Mr Pumblesnook was trying to reassure Eddie, he probably wasn't going the best way about it. Eddie now had the image of Even Madder Aunt Maud with a horse whip in her hand, and it wasn't a pretty sight.

'Then there was the time that a minor member of royalty attempted to drown me during my cameo performance in the second act of *Storm in a Teacup*. I had just –'

Eddie stopped listening after that. He was beginning to wonder whether he could get away with wearing cushion padding under his clothes on the night, without anyone noticing. (Ex-Private Drabb had done much the same when he was most recently 'volunteered' by his colleagues to take part in the beating of the bounds of the Awful End estate. In Drabb's case, it made the wizened old man look impressively muscly.)

As it was, it would turn out that his great-aunt's and uncle's reaction was one of the least of his worries on the play's opening night.

★

See that last sentence? I suspect there's a technical term for such sentences in creative writing course circles. If not, there jolly well should be. It's one of those sentences hinting at what's to come. It's also a way of saying to the reader, 'I know that there ain't much happening at the moment and it might be more fun spending a few minutes going through your old toenail clippings collection, but trust me: things really are going to liven up eventually' . . . which means that such sentences might be seen as being a bit of a cheat.

Rather than saying 'hang on in there', wouldn't it be better for an author to make every page so interesting that they don't have to resort to whetting the appetite with promises? (Whetting – with an 'h' – refers to sharpening the appetite, here, and has nothing to do with slobbering.)

On the other hand, such sentences can make you, the reader, reassess what you've just read. Take the shopping list currently attached to the fridge door (by a magnet shaped like a sticking plaster) in this house. It must have been left here by the owner.

Here's what it says:

115

Milk (full fat)
Doughnuts (chocolate)
Carrots (large sack)
Baked Beans (4-pack)
Chocolate biscuits (plain)

Now, what if I was to tell you that what makes this *particular* shopping list so interesting is that one of these items has been poisoned . . ?

Aha! Not such a boring list after all now, is it? Well, it is, the truth be told, but at least you might be wondering which the poisonous item is . . . and whether it was deliberately poisoned . . . and, if so, who the intended victim was.

Or what if I told you the person who wrote it was supposed to be on a diet? Now all that chocolate is telling a different story . . . or if the person who wrote it was having a rabbit to stay, or conducting experiments about trying to see in the dark which might – in both instances – explain the carrots . . . and how come the list is still here?

So maybe my *As-it-was-it-would-turn-out-that-his-great-aunt's-and-uncle's-reaction-was-one-of-the-least-of-his-worries-on-the-play's-opening-night* line is

116

part of a worthy tradition and doesn't deserve such contempt after all. I'll let you decide.

It's just that I didn't want to try to sneak it in under the radar.

My conscience is clear.

★

In the weeks that Eddie had been rehearsing, rehearsing, rehearsing, and watching A. C. Pryden's portrait of Mad Uncle Jack turn from a few lines on an otherwise blank canvas into a startlingly lifelike representation of his great uncle, his cousin Fabian had become a very skilled props assistant. Bless Him – sorry, it's that nickname again, of course his real name was Mr Blessing – had never really had a title before but, now that he had an assistant, things changed. He became 'Props Master'.

It wasn't only Fabian's job to make some of the props – which included coming up with ideas on what to use and how to construct them – but he also had to help source props that didn't need making. For example, one day Bless Him gave him the job of trying to create the impression that there was a hot-air balloon on stage. (Mr Pumblesnook was to play the role of Woolf Tablet, the famous photographer, in whose balloon various members of the Dickens family, accompanied by a private

117

detective – also played by Pumblesnook – had chased Eddie's kidnapper, driving a stolen hearse across the moors below.) Creating the basket of the balloon had been straightforward enough. Fabian 'borrowed' the self-same laundry basket that Dawkins had previously been trapped in. The envelope – the actual balloony part of the balloon – was a lot harder to solve and it was whilst Fabian was searching the warren of rooms in Awful End for inspiration that he saw a chandelier and realised that he could use one of the crystal baubles as a prop for the Dog's Bone Diamond.

As Fabian was crossing the driveway to the stable block, which housed the props' store, he encountered EMAM and Mad Uncle Jack walking

hand in hand. Annabelle was trotting behind them – or, at least, doing as passable an attempt at trotting as a little crocodile could – delicately holding poor Malcolm between her jaws. (Think of a faithful dog carrying a newspaper.)

'What's that you've got there, Edmund?' demanded Even Madder Aunt Maud, looking at the bauble in his hand.

'Fabian,' he corrected her.

'Don't lie to your great-aunt,' snapped Mad Uncle Jack. 'That's far too small to be Fabian.'

'Oh, this? This is from one of the chandeliers, Mad Aunt Maud –' began Fabian, breaking off as he saw an extraordinary glint appear in EMAM's eye.

'Shiny,' she said, elongating the word so that it came out as: '*Shiiiiiiiiiiiiiiiiiineeeeeeeeeeeeeeee!*' She reached out to try to touch the cut crystal.

Mad Uncle Jack grabbed her wrist. 'Go and put that thing away at once! You know full well that your great-aunt suffers from picanosis.'

Of course, Fabian *didn't* know full well that Even Madder Aunt Maud suffered from picanosis because he was Fabian, not Eddie . . . and, equally importantly, he had no idea what picanosis was either.

Because I've been unable to find any contemporary medical reference to such an ailment, I can only guess at what it was supposed to be. It's a pretty educated guess, though. Firstly, as any reader of *Terrible Times* will know, Even Madder Aunt Maud had a strange attraction to shiny things (a polished shell case and a fabulously expensive diamond, to name but two). Secondly, there are a few birds with reputations for collecting shiny things, too, including jackdaws and magpies. And the Latin name for magpie is *Pica pica*. And, thirdly, the word-ending nosis comes from the Greek *nosos*, meaning disease. See where I'm heading? I think it's a pretty safe bet that – whether made up or not by the doctor who originally diagnosed her with it – picanosis must be a form of magpie-disease or shiny-nosis.

Fabian slipped the bauble in his pocket, wished his great-aunt and great-uncle a pleasant day and hurried on his way.

Inside the stable, he expected to find Bless Him hard at work with a pot of glue or a hammer and nails turning something into something else that would look good from where the audience was sitting. Instead, he found him wrestling with a chimney-sweep.

An Old Acquaintance

*In which Eddie dodges punches
and low-flying vegetables*

Traditionally, chimney-sweeps are considered good luck, though I'm not sure why that should be. It can't have been much fun being a chimney sweep in Victorian England, particularly if you were a child, seeing as how you were often sent up the actual chimney. The description 'sooty' doesn't do justice to the state these poor boys ended up in. But lucky they were considered to be, if you followed certain rituals. According to *Old Roxbee's Book of Etiquette & Folklore*, if you came across a sweep – and he had to be in his working clothes and good 'n' dirty, or it didn't count – you had to raise your hat, or bow, or call out a cheery greeting, or (if you were of the female persuasion) curtsey.

Eddie Dickens didn't feel inclined to do any of these when he caught sight of this particular sweep, who tumbled out of the stable block, in a mass of tangled arms and legs which seemed to include his cousin Fabian and the props man.

There was much shouting and grunting, and the occasional punch was thrown by all three parties. Eddie quickly deduced that Fabian and Bless Him were on the same side, in a united front against the sweep – not that all the blows reached their intended target – so decided he should go to their aid. Three against one is always better than two against one, as the old saying goes. (Not *fairer*, just better if you're trying to win.)

Eddie launched into the mêlée and somehow managed to grab the sweep's collar which came off in his hand. It wasn't that he'd ripped the shirt, it was just that many more people wore detachable collars back then.

With Eddie now having entered the fray, the chimney-sweep admitted defeat. He simply stopped struggling and slumped, dead-weight, to the ground. 'I surrender,' he groaned.

'What did he do?' Eddie asked Fabian, helping his cousin to his feet.

Fabian shrugged. 'To tell you the truth, I don't

know,' he admitted.

'Then why were you fighting him?'

'Why were *you* fighting him?' Fabian asked Eddie in return.

'Well – er – because you were. I thought you could do with some help!'

'Well, I was helping him,' said Fabian, indicating Mr Blessing, who was yanking the chimney-sweep to his feet.

I don't want you to be under the impression that the sweep was a boy. Far from it. (Look at the picture on page 121). Though younger than the white-haired Props Master, he was old enough to be Eddie's father and then some. He was also very large. Not large in the same way that the detective (now chief-) inspector was large before his unintended diet, which was on the fat side of fat. Nor large in the sense that an escaped convict by the name of Bonecrusher – whom Eddie had once had the misfortune to meet – was large, which was on the great-big-wall-of-muscle side of large. The sweep was large-framed and stocky. Which is why it had taken three of them to calm him.

It also meant that if he didn't want to be yanked to his feet he could probably have made sure that he wasn't, but he didn't put up any resistance.

'What's going on, Mister B?' Eddie asked Bless Him.

'I found him tampering with some of the equipment,' said the Props Master, 'and when I confronted him, he came at me.'

'I did nuffink of the sort,' the sweep protested. 'I was lookin' that's all, an' you startled me.'

'A likely story!' said Bless Him who, like Eddie and Fabian, had become smeared with soot following their brief skirmish.

'Look,' said the hulk of a man. 'If I 'ave something to 'ide, why haven't I legged it outa 'ere? It ain't likes you three could stop me.'

'True,' said Eddie and Fabian, not only simultaneously but also at the same time.

'So what are you doing here, Mister –?'

'Scarple,' said Mr Scarple.

The name sounded very familiar to Eddie, though he couldn't quite place it. 'So what brings you to Awful End, Mr Scarple? I know it's not to clean chimneys. My great-uncle has his ex-privates to do that for him.'

'I'm 'ere to meet an old acquaintance, and to send greetin's from my daughter to another,' said the sweep. 'One of you lads ain't by any chance Master Edmund? Daniella never said there was two of yous.'

'Daniella!' said Eddie in amazement. Of course! That's where Eddie had heard the name Scarple before. The lovely Daniella Scarple had been the assistant to the escapologist the Great Zucchini! Despite bearing more than a passing resemblance to a horse and treating Eddie as though he were an idiot – not surprisingly, because at the outset he had become a mumbling, dribbling buffoon in her presence – Eddie had taken quite a shine to her. 'You're Daniella's father?'

The sweep put out his hand. 'I most certainly am. So you're Edmund. My daughter laughs about you still, and sends 'er best regards.'

'Is she nearby?'

Scarple shook his head. ''Er an' that man Zucchini is currently in Paris, entertainin' the crowned 'eads of Europe, or so she'd 'ave us believe.'

'A pity,' said Eddie. 'It'd have been good to see her again . . . What were you, in fact, doing when Mr Blessing came in on you?'

'Daniella 'ad told me 'ows you'd first met Zucchini in a coffin in this 'ere stable block, so I took the liberty of 'aving a quick look round before presentin' meself at the 'ouse –'

'If that's true,' said Bless Him, 'why were you tampering with the mechanism of that dagger?' One of the props which had been in the possession of Mr Pumblesnook's band of wandering theatricals for many a year was a spring-loaded dagger. When pressed against an actor, the blade

125

retracted into the handle, giving the impression that it was sinking into the victim's flesh. If anyone was to cause the blade to jam, it could give someone a nasty injury.

'I weren't tamperin',' Scarple protested. 'Just lookin', I assures you.'

'And who's the old acquaintance?' asked Fabian, who'd been busy trying to brush the soot off his clothes.

'Beg pardon?'

'You said that you were here to see an old acquaintance.'

'Oh, 'im. I'm 'ere to see a certain Gherkin. I'm sure you knows who I mean, if you've met 'im.'

'You know Gherkin!' Eddie smiled. 'It certainly is a small world.'

'It's just that I do weddin's and 'e used to do funerals. Our paths would sometimes cross in churchyards.'

'Weddings?' frowned Eddie.

'Most certainly, Master Edmund. It's considered good luck to 'ave a sweep outside the church at ya weddin'. I not only gets an 'andshake from the groom 'an a kiss from the bride but, most important of all, some money for me troubles. It's what Gherkin would describe as a lucrative sideline.'

'Do we believe him, Master Eddie?' asked Bless

126

Him, who would defer to a Dickens on the matter, but didn't want to ask Fabian because Fabian was supposed to be working under him.

'If Gherkin can vouch for Mr Scarple, then everything's fine by me . . . Forgive our less than friendly welcome, Mr Scarple.'

'A misundertandin', that's all,' said the sweep. He limped back into the stable block to retrieve his battered top hat from the floor of the props room, where it had fallen at the outbreak of the scuffle. The condition of the hat didn't bother him in the slightest. It had been second- or third-hand when he'd first acquired it, and had been battered even then.

Fabian went back to work on the props with Bless Him, whilst Eddie led the limping chimney-sweep to the summerhouse which had become Gherkin's home since the day he'd arrived. Back in the days of Dr Malcontent Dickens, the summerhouse had been furnished with kiddie-sized tables and chairs for his three young sons. Even the shelving and door handles were at a lower height, which made it the ideal bedroom and sitting room for the dwarf, who still took his meals and bathed in the main house (though not at the same time).

Eddie and Scarple found Gherkin reading a book.

'Harry!' said Gherkin, obviously delighted to see him.

STOP. Wait a minute. Before I type another line, I should make it absolutely clear that Harry Scarple was not – I repeat NOT – the Harry (aka 'arry) in the Prologue and the (illegal) intermission on pages 106, 107 and 108. In books and films it's quite rare for characters to have the same name – probably to avoid confusion – but in real life, it's quite a different matter. Glad to be of service.

Gherkin shook Scarple's hand warmly. 'What brings you to this neck of the woods?' he asked.

'I've been cleaning them chimneys over at Lamberley 'all. Old Jim Langham who used to do them is now Jim long-gone, an' the job's been passed on to me.'

'Old Jim's loss is your gain,' said Gherkin.

'I raised a pint of thrupenny gargle* to his memory,' said the sweep. 'It's good to see you, Gherkin. I 'eard you was workin' for Mad Mr Dickens now, and Master Eddie is an ol' friend of me daughter, Daniella, so I thought I'd kill two birds with one stone by payin' a visit to Awful End.'

Gherkin turned to Eddie, eyebrow raised. 'You know Daniella?'

Eddie nodded. 'It's a long story,' he said.

'I would very much like to hear it sometime,' said Gherkin.

'I'd be delighted to tell you,' said Eddie.

'By all accounts, it were quite an adventure,' said Daniella's father.

'Where are my manners? Sit down! Sit down!' urged Gherkin.

There was only one adult-sized chair, and Scarple lowered himself into it, left leg stuck out stiffly.

---

* a particularly strong and unpleasant-tasting drink

Eddie perched himself on the edge of a small table. 'Were you injured during our fight?' he asked with concern.

'Fight?' asked the dwarf.

'A misunderstanding, is all,' Scarple explained quickly. 'No, Eddie. I've been a chimney sweep man and boy and 'ave sustained more injuries than is good for any of God's creatures.'

Once again, Eddie was reminded what a sheltered life he led as a child of the upper classes . . . or *would* have led if he hadn't kept on finding himself the centre of some extraordinary events. Things had been remarkably peaceful these past few months.

His thoughts were interrupted by a distant dull thud, followed by a dreadful 'CRASH!' as something the size of a cannonball came hurtling through the closed door of the summerhouse, glass shattering and wood splintering in its wake.

Eddie and Gherkin threw themselves to the ground in an instant. Scarple was less speedy but, fortunately the projectile missed him by a stoat's whisker and hit the back wall of the summerhouse with enough force to cause the pictures to shake on all the walls.

'We're under attack!' said Scarple in amazement. He struggled to his feet and joined the other two on the floor.

130

'What on Earth –?' said Gherkin.

'It could be nothing to worry about,' said Eddie.

'Nuffink to worry about? I coulda been killed!' protested Scarple.

'I mean that we may not be under attack, Mr Scarple,' said Eddie. 'It could simply be another of my great-uncle or great-aunt's harebrained schemes. There could be a perfectly – er – simple explanation.'

A second or so later, there was another distant thud, and another projectile came into view, heading in the direction of the summerhouse.

'Heads down!' shouted the dwarf, putting his head in his hands and rolling himself into a ball.

This time, the object landed on the grass just short of the summer house.

Eddie got into a crouching position and made it over to the shattered door. He peered outside. 'It appears to be a cabbage.'

'A cabbage?'

'A cabbage,' said Eddie.

'Someone is firing cabbages at us?' asked Harry Scarple.

'It would appear so,' said Eddie.

The chimney sweep stood up and retrieved the projectile which had caused so much damage. 'Yup, this one is certainly a cabbage too.'

'Keep down, Scarple!' said Gherkin. 'A cabbage

fired at this speed could still take your head off.'
Gherkin wasn't wrong. A candle fired from a
shotgun can pass through a wooden door, so why
not fire a cabbage from a cannon or a giant
catapult . . . apart from the fact that it would be a
ridiculous thing to do, of course.

'I suggest we retreat!' says Gherkin, 'But keep
low!'

Gingerly trying to avoid the shards of broken
glass scattered across the floor, the three of them
pushed open one of the tattered doors and dashed,
still crouching, across a stretch of lawn into the
cover of a nearby shrubbery. The third cabbage
came smashing into the summerhouse moments
later.

Episode 12

A Blast from the Past

In which matters turn from worse
to even worse, which can't be good

Eddie didn't waste any time. Whilst Scarple and Gherkin were still recovering from the shock of it all, he was skirting through the undergrowth, heading in the direction from which the cabbages had been fired, as fast as his legs could carry him. He tripped once, having caught his foot in a tree root, and scraped his skin against some particularly spiky leaves of some foreign specimen, but this barely slowed him down.

When Eddie broke his cover, bursting from the undergrowth onto the upper lawn, he didn't know what to find. He could be forgiven for thinking that MUJ or EMAM might have been behind the firing of cabbages at the summerhouse. If any of the household were going to undertake such an action, it was more than likely to be them; or some of the ex-privates following their instructions. But it wasn't.

With preparations for the play under way, it had also crossed Eddie's mind that the sudden onslaught of low-flying cabbages might be the testing of a prop which had somehow gone wrong. Eddie's father, Mr Dickens, had, as you may recall, included a few scenes set aboard *The Pompous Pig*. You may also recall my telling you that he embellished the truth in places (which is another way of saying he made things up). Although there were no cannons aboard the vessel, Laudanum Dickens had the character of first mate, Mr Briggs, firing one at the fleeing Swags. So, again, it might be reasonable to suppose that it was Bless Him or Fabian or someone testing such a cannon, either real or home-made. But it wasn't.

There before him was indeed the props cannon – which had been delivered *after* the Dickenses had repelled Stinky Hoarebacker's hunt, or it might well have been pressed into service by the defending army – but the person busy loading another cabbage into the menacing barrel was a stranger to Eddie.

Eddie had hoped the commotion might have brought others to the scene because he wasn't yet sure whether he was about to deal with someone who was firing vegetables for a bit of fun, unaware of the damage and endangerment to human life . . . or whether this small round man was intent on serious harm.

'STOP!' shouted Eddie running towards the man.

The man did nothing of the sort. Cabbage now loaded, he began fiddling with what Eddie knew to be the fuse. The man tried unsuccessfully to suppress a worrying giggle. The resulting sound was even more worrying.

'There are people down there!' shouted Eddie, pointing in the direction he'd just come. 'You might kill someone!'

'HA!' shouted the man. 'HA! I say. HA! to you and HA! to them. HA! I say!'

'Help!' shouted Eddie. 'Somebody! Anybody!' He had once been told that the best way to attract people's attention when you needed help was to shout 'Fire!'. But he wasn't about to risk this when standing by a man with a cannon. 'Help!' shouted Eddie. 'Father! Dawkins! Uncle Jack! Anyone!' He waved his arms around frantically.

As well as genuinely seeking assistance, Eddie was also trying to let the rotund stranger know that there were plenty of people about, and to disorient him with noise and movement.

What should I do? What should I do? thought Eddie. So long as I'm not standing in front of the cannon, I should be safe. Should I jump on him? Tackle him? Although Eddie was as sure as he could be that he'd never met the man before, there was something strangely familiar about this stranger. He reminded Eddie of someone . . . or something. That was it! Of course!

'Peevance!' shouted Eddie. 'Is that you?'

The man was clearly startled. He hesitated and, in that moment, skinny saucer-eyed Eddie bravely launched himself at the man –

– and let's leave him there in mid-air for a moment whilst I remind those who've read *Dubious Deeds* and tell those who haven't, who and what Peevance was. Lance Peevance was originally the name of a man (a hard-working schoolteacher, in fact) whom Mad Uncle Jack had spotted in town on a number of occasions. Mr Peevance was rather round and knobbly and, to most eyes, an unfortunately ugly man. Later, Lance Peevance also became the name of a hybrid vegetable which looked like a very large, knobbly pea. Mad Uncle Jack had been the creator of said vegetable and had also been the one to name it. The instant it grew, it reminded MUJ so strongly of the teacher, that he went to the trouble of finding out the man's identity, and named his creation after him. Mr

Peevance was far from happy about this and, very foolishly, took Mad Uncle Jack to court over the matter. I say foolishly because not only was MUJ a gentleman and Peevance was not, but MUJ also lived up at the big house, which meant that no local court would dare find him guilty of anything. Technically, of course, Lamberley Hall was the really big house in those parts, but it was built with 'new money' and its occupants were a couple of sisters*, and women really didn't count in the same way.

The outcome was that the human Lance Peevance was crippled by costs and fled to the Continent.** He was eventually caught in France and brought back to England, a debtor and a ruined man.

The vegetables retained his name and Mad Uncle Jack still grew them once in a while. Eddie had heard the story and seen the vegetables many times, which was how he finally recognised the man, at whom he now launched himself –

– and, sadly, missed, landing winded on the grass beside him. The cannon fired for a fourth time and, what had been a distant thud to him on the three previous occasions was much more of a

* the Andrews sisters with a small 's', of course
** disguised as a bag of coal, somewhat surprisingly

loud 'WUMPH!' close to, though certainly not a bang.

The man started kicking Eddie as he lay there which is as horrible as it sounds. Eddie had always felt rather sorry for the schoolteacher whenever he had heard the story. He knew how exasperating his family could be and, on top of that, the poor man had lost his job and home and everything . . . but being kicked by someone can rather change your opinion of them.

As Eddie tried to grab Peevance's leg the next time it took a swing at him, four other pairs of legs came into view. Two of them were decidedly short and green and belonged to Annabelle. The other two pairs belonged to Mad Uncle Jack and Even Madder Aunt Maud.

'Help me!' shouted Eddie. 'It's Lance Peevance!'

'You're mistaken, Edmund,' said Mad Uncle Jack, picking up one of the cabbages stacked next to the cannon. 'It's a common or garden cabbage.'

'No, *him*!' shouted Eddie, who now had the ex-schoolteacher standing on top of him.

'No, I don't know him,' said MUJ. 'And I'm not sure I want to.'

Lance Peevance was eyeing his arch nemesis with such hatred that it looked as if his eyes might actually burst into flames.

Eddie tried to get to his feet, but – without taking his eyes off MUJ for one moment – Peevance trod on him. Hard. 'Help me, Aunt Maud,' Eddie managed.

EMAM slapped Peevance on the back. 'Excellent costume, Mr Pumblesnook,' she said. 'Wonderful make-up!'

'Help me!' rasped Eddie a second time.

'Keeping in character? Good boy, Edmund,' said his great aunt. 'Mr Pumblesnook has taught you well.'

Eddie felt like throttling her.

It seemed Peevance had similar thoughts regarding Mad Uncle Jack. 'I'm going to kill you, Dickens!' said Peevance, using Eddie as a launch pad to land on MUJ's back, hands around his throat.

MUJ fell to the ground in an angular tangle of jutting-out elbows and knees. He looked like a daddy-long-legs in distress.

Even Madder Aunt Maud was outraged. 'My

Jack isn't in your stupid play!' she snapped. She went to beat the man she took to be Mr Pumblesnook with Malcolm . . . but she wasn't carrying him. She looked to Annabelle, and she wasn't carrying him either. Now she wasn't sure what to do. It was obvious from his sticking out tongue and bulging eyes that her dear, sweet Jack didn't particularly like being strangled. And the sudden discovery of the absence of her stuffed stoat caused EMAM such anguish that it completely knocked the wind out of her sails.

Battered and bruised, Eddie struggled to his feet and was about to throw himself on Peevance a second time, when help arrived.

It arrived in the form of Scarple and Gherkin. In next to no time, Scarple was sitting on Mr Peevance, pinning down his arms and legs, whilst Gherkin was tying him up with some bunting.

'Are you all right, Eddie?' asked the chimney-sweep.

'I'll be fine,' said Eddie.

'Who is this madman?' asked Gherkin as he tied another knot.

'My husband, Jack,' said Even Madder Aunt Maud. 'I believe you've already met.'

Gherkin did his eyebrow raising thing again.

'I think you'll find he's a Mr Lance Peevance,' said Eddie. 'He has a grudge against the family.'

'By Jove!' said MUJ. 'You're right! It is that rascal Peevance.' He turned to their captive. 'Aren't you supposed to be in jail?'

Suddenly, there was a cry of 'CHARGE!' and the small gathering found themselves surrounded by members of Mr Pumblesnook's ragtag group of wandering theatricals – including Mr Pumblesnook and his good lady wife, but with the exception of Bless Him and Fabian – each brandishing a weapon of sorts, ranging from newspaper cucumbers to a genuine sword, a table leg and a garden rake. Dawkins was there too, brandishing a rolling pin. Gibbering Jane was also on the scene, brandishing baby Oliphant, who was brandishing his silver rattle. The ex-privates were also in attendance. They all formed a tight circle around the cannon.

Dressed in resplendent uniform, and waving a sabre, Mr Pumblesnook pushed himself to the fore. 'It would seem that you gentlemen have everything under control,' he said.

Better late than never, thought Eddie.

'Apologies for the delay,' said Pumblesnook, 'but I thought it best to be correctly dressed for a rescue of such great importance.'

Eddie had to admit that he did look splendid.

Whilst everyone fussed over Mad Uncle Jack (*I'm fine! Fine! Had worse happen every day when I*

141

was fighting the Hoolers**), helped the distraught Even Madder Aunt Maud in her search for Malcolm (*'If anyone's so much as harmed a hair on his beautiful head, they'll have me to answer to!'*) or assisted with the hauling off of poor old Lance Peevance (*'HA! You've not heard the last of me, you Dickenses! No jail cell can hold me!'*), Eddie slipped away. He wanted to nurse his wounds in private.

As he mounted the first few steps of Awful End's main staircase, A. C. Pryden came hurrying down. 'Eddie!' he said. 'Terrible, terrible news. Please follow me,' and he turned and ran up again, two or three stairs at a time.

Eddie followed the artist into his bedroom. In the corner stood a canvas covered by the familiar curtain on the easel. Now that MUJ's portrait had been completed, Pryden kept it in here rather than his makeshift studio downstairs.

'Lift the curtain,' said Pryden.

Eddie obeyed. Underneath was a blank canvas.

'Stolen,' said A. C. Pryden. 'The painting's been stolen!'

---

* Not some foreign tribe, but former neighbours

Eddie on the Case!

*In which Eddie sees some familiar faces
in some unfamiliar places*

'Stolen?' gasped Mr Dickens. 'Are you sure?'
'You didn't – er – hide the painting by any
chance, father, did you?' asked Eddie.

'Surely you're not accusing your father of being
a thief?' demanded Mrs Dickens.

'Not at all, mother,' said Eddie hurriedly. 'It's
just that I thought you might have – er – put the
painting aside until after Monday night's first
performance of the play, so that the unveiling of
Mad Uncle Jack's portrait didn't –' He tried to
remember his father's exact words '– steal our
thunder.'

'No, I did not,' said his father indignantly.

'You don't think Jack or Maud could have taken it, do you, Laudanum?' asked Mrs Dickens.

'I do not!' snapped Mr Dickens, in a tone of voice which suggested that he couldn't imagine MUJ or EMAM ever doing something strange like that.

'And they both have an alibi,' said Eddie.

'A laundry basket?' said his mother.

Eddie thought for a moment. 'I think you're thinking of an ali baba, mother,' he said. 'I said alibi. I mean that a number of people can vouch for where they were when Mad Uncle Jack's portrait was slipped for the blank canvas. Including me.'

According to A. C. Pryden, he had knocked the easel when opening the flap in the desk in his room in order to write a letter, and the curtain had fallen from it, revealing the picture beneath. He had replaced the curtain and, finding that he'd run out of writing paper, went downstairs to get some which he'd seen on a writing table in the drawing room. Whilst in the drawing room, he'd looked through the window and witnessed the antics at the bottom of the top lawn, involving Eddie, Peevance and the others. His short time at Awful End had taught him one thing: DON'T GET INVOLVED. He went back upstairs to write his letter. He'd been gone from his room for less than ten minutes.

Just as he was about to sit down at his desk, he noticed something strange – he had an artist's eye for things, remember. The curtain over the painting was the wrong way up. Technically, of course, there was no right way or wrong way. There was no pattern on the curtain, and the hem was the same on all four sides. It was just that the thick material had a pile: brush it in one direction and it lay beautifully flat. Brush against the pile and it stuck up. Pryden always hung the curtain so that the pile could be smoothed downwards. Puzzled, he lifted the curtain. The painting had gone, and the thief's only window of opportunity had been the ten minutes or so that he'd been away from the room.

'Has he sent for the police?' asked Eddie's father.

'No,' said Eddie. 'He doesn't want anyone to know yet, father. Not even the police. You must promise not to tell anybody. No-one. Both of you, please.'

'My lips are sealed,' Mr Dickens reassured him.

'*Fow aw moy,*' said his mother, which was mouth-full-of-ball bearings for 'so are mine'.

'Thank you,' said Eddie. 'It's just that it's a little – er – embarrassing for him. He doesn't want the War Office to get wind of it until he's exhausted all other avenues. Those were his very words.'

'What does he plan to do, hire a private investigator?' Mr Dickens asked.

'No, not yet,' said Eddie, whose own experience of a private investigator hadn't been an entirely happy one.

Now that Eddie had spoken to his parents, and believed that they genuinely knew nothing about it, he returned to Mr Pryden's room.

He found the artist sitting on his bed, holding the large blank canvas across his lap. He looked up as Eddie entered the room.

'This must have been a carefully planned theft with someone who had inside information,' said Eddie.

'How did you work that out?' Pryden asked.

146

'The canvas,' said Eddie. 'It's exactly the same size as the painting they replaced under the curtain.'

'Which means that someone must have seen and measured the original and had it made especially!' said the painter, in that penguiny way of his. 'This was no spur of the moment thing. It was carefully plotted –'

'Which means that the whole Mr Peevance firing the cabbages from the cannon could have been *a diversion*!'

'I suppose he could have been a decoy,' said Pryden. He didn't sound convinced.

'But how could they have got him to play his part?' said Eddie. 'I'm afraid Mr Peevance appears to have – er – lost control . . . I seriously doubt he could have been following orders.'

'An unwitting accomplice?' said the painter.

'Does anyone know how he got out of jail, and from the jail to here?' asked Eddie. 'Where did he get those cabbages from? How did he know that there was a cannon here in the first place?'

'We'll never know,' said Pryden.

'You could try asking him,' Eddie suggested.

'How?' asked the painter. 'I thought the peelers had carted him off to the local police station whilst they decide what to do with him next.'

'Exactly,' said Eddie. 'You can speak to him there.'

'The peelers will want to know why, and I really want to keep this our secret –'

'Then we won't ask them,' said Eddie.

*

Eddie was familiar with the cells in the basement of the local constabulary, and knew that each had a little barred window which was at ankle-height with the pavement outside (not that pavements have ankles). Eddie crouched down and looked into the first cell. There was an extremely large woman, smelling of grog – even from where Eddie was – and snoring loudly. He moved on to the next window. This revealed a man dressed as a cleric, playing a game of patience on a rickety table, with home-made cards. (Based on information gleaned from local papers of the time, it seems likely that this was Barnaby Hawthorne, the notorious con artist whose speciality was tricking ladies of a certain age to part with their money. His *modus operandi* was to dress as a clergyman of some description or other, in order to gain their trust more quickly.)

The third cell housed two men, both in handcuffs, sitting glaring at each other from opposite sides of the room. Through the fourth barred window, Eddie saw the back view of the unmistakeable figure of Lance Peevance.

'He's in there,' said Eddie, straightening up.

'Good luck.' He and A. C. Pryden had agreed that there was no point in him trying to talk to Peevance. Not only because of their confrontation by the cannon but also because it would now be obvious to the ex-school teacher that Eddie was one of the dreaded Dickenses. Pryden would have a far better chance of getting information from the man. 'I'll walk the streets and keep an eye out for peelers.'

'I'm still not sure about this,' said Pryden.

'There's nothing to lose,' Eddie reminded him.

The artist crouched by the window. He stuck his head up against the bars. 'Psssst! Peevance!' he whispered.

Eddie wandered to the corner of the building and looked both ways down the street. He tried to look as casual as possible when the desk sergeant strode purposefully down the steps of the police station and across the road. The policeman entered a small bow-fronted shop named TRUMBLES, emerging soon after with a large paper bag.

When the sergeant recrossed the street, Eddie turned away and pretended to be interested in a horse-drawn open-topped omnibus which was approaching from the opposite direction. His interest became genuine when he saw a familiar face sitting on the top deck: it was Daniella's chimney-sweep father. Then he recognised the man he was talking to. The bandaged head should have been a clue. It was Doctor 'Moo-Cow' Moot. How curious, thought Eddie. What are Scarple and Moot doing travelling on a bus together? Doctors and chimney sweeps didn't mix in ordinary society except perhaps, as Eddie had so recently learnt, at weddings.

Eddie put his hand in his pocket and pulled out a handful of pennies, ha'pennies and a farthing, which was more than enough for a bus fare. He was tempted to jump on the vehicle as it came to a halt a few yards away, and passengers hopped on and off. The only thing which stopped him was that he was on lookout duty for Mr Pryden.

The desk sergeant now back inside the station – probably behind his beloved desk – and the omnibus now moving off down the street, Eddie went back around the corner to check up on Pryden. There was no sign of him. Eddie hurried down the pavement and glanced through the tiny barred window into the ex-schoolteacher's cell. Peevance was lying face-down on the large wooden bench set into the wall below, which was used as a bed. He appeared to be chewing his pillow, or more tearing at it with his teeth. Eddie could hear ripping sounds between Lance Peevance's anguished mutterings, and the odd stray feather fluttered about the cell.

Eddie guessed that A. C. Pryden's conversation

with him hadn't gone too well . . . but where was the artist now? Eddie straightened up and went in search of him, wanting to tell him about the strange sight of a well-to-do doctor in an exclusive practice talking with Scarple, as thick as thieves . . . *Thieves.* Were they somehow involved in the theft of the painting? If so – and if Peevance really had been some kind of a diversion – it can't all have gone to plan. The possibility of Scarple's head being blown off by a cabbage cannonball had been a very real one.

Eddie had been so deep in thought that he almost walked slap-bang into a lamppost and, in avoiding it at the last moment, stepped on the foot of a child hurrying past him.

'I beg your pardon,' said Eddie. The child said nothing, just kept on moving. Eddie turned to watch him go, realising that this was no child after all. Sure, the figure was dressed in a sailor suit and carrying a lollipop almost as big as his head, but Eddie would have recognised the distinctive body shape and spritely walk anywhere. It was Gherkin the dwarf!

Eddie almost called out his name, but stopped himself just in time. It was obvious that the man hadn't wanted to be recognised. With A. C. Pryden nowhere in sight, there was nothing to stop Eddie following someone this time.

Gherkin, outsized lollipop in hand, was now skipping down the street. Despite his ridiculous outfit, Eddie thought it unlikely that anyone looking at his face would be fooled into thinking that he was a child for one minute. It wasn't only a man's face but a fairly *old* man's face at that. Then again, he was way below most adults' eye level, and people didn't generally pay much attention to children. *And* he's probably using that lollipop to hide behind, thought Eddie.

Gherkin passed the police station, the post office and a shop selling everything you ever needed for riding and looking after horses (except, perhaps for stables, which would have been difficult to store out at the back). Taking a quick look from left to right – not noticing Eddie who had positioned himself behind two conveniently large women who were deep in conversation about the merits of a certain type of hat ribbon – he darted down a narrow alley. Eddie waited a moment, then nipped over to the entrance, peered around it and, seeing that the coast was clear, hurried down the alley himself, just in time to see Gherkin disappear through a large door. When Eddie reached it, he could make out faded lettering on the wood. What did it say?

I ATE PROPER Y

'I ate proper y'. *Who* ate proper y? What was proper y anyway? And was there such a thing as *im*proper y, Eddie wondered. Then it occurred to him that it might originally have read 'I ATE PROPERLY', like someone was announcing that they'd eaten a decent meal.

It was then, and only then, that Eddie realised that what the writing must have originally said was: PRIVATE PROPERTY. Feeling the tiniest bit foolish, Eddie gave the door a push. It wouldn't budge. Now what? he wondered.

He would've liked to have dragged an old packing crate under a window and have climbed up on it to take a look inside. The problem was twofold, though: there was neither a packing crate nor a window. The handleless door was set into a blank brick wall. The wall was only blank in the sense that there were no windows in it. It wasn't blank like the canvas that had been switched for A. C. Pryden's portrait of Mad Uncle Jack. There was an advertisement painted directly onto the brickwork which read:

ALWAYS USE
OLD ROXBEE'S
SAFETY MATCHES.

It looked like it had been there a long time, but that – unlike the writing on the door – the black lettering had been regularly touched up with paint to keep it looking fresh.

Eddie was no expert on the subtleties of advertising but, the more he looked at it, the more puzzled he was by this advertisement. Firstly, most advertisements painted on the side of buildings were painted high up for all to see, not at chest and head height. Secondly, such adverts were usually painted on main roads or at least where lots of passers-by would pass by . . . not down some narrow little alleyway.

Eddie was beginning to wonder whether he was seeing mysteries where none existed. Maybe there was a perfectly good reason for Dr Moot to have been on a bus, rather than in his pony and trap, speaking to Scarple. And what business of Eddie's was it if Gherkin dressed as a child? He'd worked in a team of tumblers hadn't he? And they must have worn costumes . . . Maybe he'd always played the role of a youngster in 'The Remarkably Small Garfields', and wore the outfit occasionally, whilst hankering after the good old days?

Eddie heard a sound, and managed to duck into another doorway, just as the door by the Old Roxbee's safety match advert swung open. Gherkin emerged, clutching a brown paper parcel under his left arm. He nipped back down the alley the way he'd come. Once the dwarf had reached the street and turned left, in the opposite direction to the police station, Eddie broke his cover and ran up the alley after him.

Eddie found that he was very good at not being noticed. The moment he sensed or suspected that Gherkin might be about to look around, Eddie would duck into a doorway, or look into a shop window, or obscure himself behind an object or person and, on one occasion, a sheep on a lead, which tried to bite him. Its owner – a smartly dressed haughty woman whose expression seemed to dare him to ask her what on Earth she was doing taking a sheep for a walk – scowled at him, which seemed to suggest that he shouldn't tempt Isobel (her name was engraved on a tag on her collar) by putting his biteable human body so close to the animal's teeth. Remembering some Scottish police sheep of yesteryear, Eddie wondered why no one reminded sheep the world over that they were supposed to be herbivores, but his mind was soon back on his task.

Eddie suspected that Gherkin might have recognised him when he'd stepped on the dwarf's foot by the side of the police station, but didn't think that he knew that he was following him. Gherkin – whatever he was up to – was being generally cautious, rather than watching out for Eddie in particular.

They were nearing the eastern outskirts of the town now, where there were far fewer pedestrians on the pavements, more trees and less traffic on the roads. Gherkin, who'd been moving at a pace which had left Eddie a little breathless, now came to a halt at the corner of Corncrake Avenue and the Lamberley Road. Eddie looked at the house on the corner. He recognised it immediately. It had been the home and medical practice of the late Dr Humple, but the brand new brass plaque screwed onto the brick and plaster gate post read: DR SAMUEL MOOT.

All roads lead to Moo-Cow Moot, thought Eddie, wondering what would happen next.

Gherkin had been busy unwrapping the brown-paper parcel. From it he produced what appeared to be a very large stick of dynamite.

Den of Thieves

*In which Eddie sees various acquaintances
in a different light*

I expect many of you have heard of the Nobel Prize for Peace, and some of you may also have heard of other Nobel Prizes, including the Nobel Prize for Literature. (I wonder how long before I have to go to Stockholm and accept that little award? Perhaps I should start on my acceptance speech just as soon as I've finished this book.) I expect far fewer of you knew that the prizes are named after Alfred Nobel, the Swedish inventor of dynamite. (I know YOU knew, I was talking about the others.)

The story goes that, feeling guilty about the death and destruction his explosive invention caused – which had many peaceful applications, including mining – he decided to give large sums of money to recognise the higher achievements of Mankind with a capital M (which, in Swedish is Mänskligheten with a capital M). Which would all be very interesting if what Eddie could see Gherkin holding was the stick of dynamite it appeared to be.

Eddie's first thought was to go straight back to the police station to get help. By the time he'd run all the way back there, managed to convince someone to take him seriously – some of the peelers Eddie had met over the years weren't the most shining examples of the human race – and had then run all the way back *here* again, however, it would be far too late. Gherkin would have done whatever it was he was going to do. Eddie should have known that there was something odd about an official mourner who'd been given a card by Mad Uncle Jack forty or fifty (or however many years) ago it had been, suddenly turning up out of the blue like that. The trouble was, living with such a potty family, it was easy to forget what *normal* behaviour was. A dwarf dressed as a child with what appeared to be a huge lollipop in one hand and a stick of dynamite in the other could only be classed as normal by Dickens family standards.

With the remarkable agility of an ex-acrobat, Gherkin leapt over the side wall into Dr Moot's front garden. There was a rustling through the laurel bushes, like ripples on the surface of water hinting at hidden activity below, then he appeared beneath a large bay window. The only difference was that he was now holding a match in his right hand instead of the lolly. He lit the fuse.

'NO!!!' shouted Eddie, running through the gate. 'STOP!'

This didn't have the desired effect. The opposite, in fact. An angry looking man threw open the bottom sash window in the middle of the bay, and demanded. 'What's the meanin' of this?'

And Gherkin took the opportunity to throw the stick into the house, fuse burning. Eddie, meanwhile, threw himself to the pavement, waiting for the bang . . .

. . . that never came. The room, however, began to fill with smoke. It billowed from the window in great clouds. The front door flew open and the angry man, the bandaged Doctor Moot and Harry Scarple ran down the stairs. Before the first man's foot touched the garden path, Gherkin had jumped up, caught the windowsill and back-flipped up and in through the open window.

To say that Eddie's head was in a spin would be like saying that an ostrich is slightly larger than the average chicken. He didn't know who to trust or what to think, so he decided the best thing to do was to hide. He dived into a bush in the garden

159

next door, just before the three men dashed out onto the pavement; which was when he got his next surprise.

'Sssssh!' said a voice, with great authority.

Eddie turned in amazement to find that Detective Chief Inspector Bunyon had claimed the hiding place before him. (Weren't you wondering if he might turn up? I certainly was.)

Eddie ssssh-ed.

'Who threw the bomb, did you see?' spluttered Scarple.

'Na,' said the angry man. 'There was a saucer-eyed kid out 'ere shoutin', but 'e didn't throw nuffink.' He coughed a bit.

'That'll be Eddie – young Edmund Dickens,' said the chimney-sweep.

'You don't think he –?'

'He don't know nothing, Moot, calm down . . . and that weren't no bomb, Thunk.'

Thunk? thought Eddie. Who's Thunk? Has a fourth man come out of the house?

'Then what was it 'arry? 'Cos I'd say old Moot's 'ouse 'as gone up in smoke!' said Scarple.

Just a minute, thought Eddie. I thought Scarple's name was Harry, and why is this other Harry calling him Thunk?

'It's an hincendiary device, that's what that is,' said Harry, the angry man.

160

'An hincendiary device?'

'An incendiary device,' said Doctor Moot. 'Something which starts fires.'

'Well, it's certainly done that,' said Scarple.

''Ere, 'old on! I ain't so sure, Thunk. 'Ave you actually seen any flames?'

'Well, I've seen plenty of smoke, 'arry, and there's ain't no smoke without fire!'

'Harry's right!' gasped Moot. 'We've been tricked! Come on!'

'Where?'

'Back inside, of course!'

'Are you mad, Moot? You're supposed to run outa burnin' buildin's. Not into 'em!'

There was a sound of footsteps as the three men ran back up the black-and-white tiled garden path.

'Stay put,' Detective Chief Inspector Bunyon whispered in Eddie's ear. Eddie repositioned himself so that a particularly spiky branch stopped jabbing him so painfully in the ribs but, apart from that, stayed right where he was. So did the policeman. Even from his cramped position, Eddie could tell that the detective chief inspector had gained an impressive amount of weight since he'd last seen him, but was still nowhere as large as he'd been during their first encounter. Still, it was fortunate that it was such a large bush.

They sat in silence for a while. No one appeared

to come in or out again but, through the leaves, Eddie could see Harry Scarple opening some of the ground floor windows to let the smoke escape.

Eventually, Bunyon spoke. 'Time we made our exit,' he said. 'Follow me.' He crawled out of the bush on his hands and knees, and – still in this position, crawled out through the gate of Dr Moot's neighbour, and onto the pavement. Eddie did the same. A revolver fell from the detective's pocket.

Without a word, he picked it up and slipped it back inside his checked jacket. 'This way,' he said. They crawled along the pavement, further from the medical practice. When Bunyon deemed that they were a safe enough distance, he stood up, dusting down his trousers. Eddie removed a twig from his hair. A passing group of philosophers eyed them suspiciously.

'Good afternoon,' they said as one.

'Good afternoon,' said the detective chief inspector. He led Eddie to the corner of Wisteria Road where a covered carriage was waiting. 'Get in,' he said.

No sooner had Eddie shut the door than the horse trotted off. He – Eddie, not the horse (which was a *she* called Moonlight, anyway) – had a whole host of questions to ask the policeman.

Bunyon obviously guessed as much, and put up his hand for silence. 'I don't know what you thought you saw back there, Master Dickens, but one thing you can be sure of is that nothing is what it seems.'

'What I do know I saw was a dwarf calling himself Gherkin, dressed as a child, throw what looked like a stick of dynamite – which he got from a building a stone's throw from your own police station, sir – but which may have been some kind of smoke bomb, and –'

'It was a modified plumber's mate,' said Bunyon, as the carriage went over a bump.

Now, you might be forgiven for thinking that a plumber's mate was someone who held the plumber's bag of plumbery tools for him, or went for a drink with him after a hard day of strangling pipes, but you'd be wrong. What Bunyon was refering to was a plumber's smoke rocket. Those of you familiar with Victorian plumbing methods and readers of the first Sherlock Holmes short story, *A Scandal in Bohemia*, will know that a plumber's smoke-rocket was a kind of smoke bomb fired up pipes to reveal holes (the smoke coming out of them). In the aforementioned story, Sherlock Holmes sets one off to trick a woman into thinking her house is on fire so that she'll rescue an important photograph, thus revealing its hidden whereabouts.

'They make very effective smoke bombs,' said the detective.

'But why?' asked Eddie. 'And –' He stopped. The detective had obviously positioned himself in the bush before Gherkin had arrived. He knew exactly what Gherkin had thrown through the window. He'd been *expecting* him. 'How did you know this was going to happen?'

'How did I know this was going to happen?' asked Bunyon.

164

'How did you know this was going to happen?' repeated Eddie.

'A good policeman has plenty of underworld informants,' said Bunyon, 'People who'll sell their own mothers for the price of a drink.'

Eddie thought for a moment. 'I don't think any underworld informant told you about Gherkin. I think he's working for you!'

Detective Chief Inspector Bunyon glared at Eddie. 'Think he's working for me? We do have height requirements in the police force, Master Dickens, and I can assure you that your Mr Gherkin wouldn't reach them.'

'Maybe he's not exactly a policeman,' Eddie suggested, 'simply someone you can use when you need an acrobat who can get through small spaces.'

The chief inspector smiled. 'An acrobat who can get through small spaces . . .'

'I really think you owe it to me to tell me, sir. I've already been in a fight with Mr Scarple, or Thunk, or whatever his name is . . . I've been fired on in a summerhouse, with cabbages. I've been kicked and jumped on by Mr Peevance –'

Eddie was interrupted by a cry of, 'There he is, sir,' by the driver, and the cab slowed to a halt.

The door opened and Gherkin scrambled in. He looked at Eddie. 'I thought that was you outside the house. You could have ruined everything. What were you –?'

'He followed you,' said Bunyon.

'He can't have!'

'I did,' said Eddie.

The dwarf didn't know whether to be annoyed, or embarrassed or impressed, so he was all three.

'Dr Moot, Harry Scarple and that other man called Harry all have something to do with Mr Pryden's stolen painting, don't they?' said Eddie.

The detective chief inspector looked at Gherkin. Gherkin looked at the detective chief inspector. They both turned to Eddie. 'What stolen painting?' they asked.

The Final Act

*In which the curtain rises
and the plot is revealed*

That had been Friday. It was now Monday evening and, after over a month of preparation and rehearsal, Mr Dickens's play was ready for its opening night performance. After much deliberation, and a last-minute change of mind, he had entitled it *That's My Boy*. Dawkins had been sent to the local printer to give him the change of title. Unfortunately, Eddie's father hadn't written it down, and Dawkins delivered the message verbally. Unfortunate because, after years of working amongst the clatter of printing presses, Mr Sodkin was a little hard of hearing. The posters and programme came back with the title *That's*

Mabel, and there was nothing much anyone could do about it.

Mr Pumblesnook had suggested that they might make a few last-minute changes to the script, making one of the orphans Mabel, but Eddie's father had argued that this would simply confuse matters, giving the character undue importance. Fabian had come up with the idea that they could write a whole new scene at the beginning in which Eddie's parents – played by Mr and Mrs Pumblesnook – decide that if they have a girl they'll call her Mabel, and if it's a boy they'll call him Edmund. 'But when Eddie's born they still mistakenly call him Mabel once in a while.' Laudanum Dickens hadn't been keen on that idea either. In the end, they left the play unaltered and had Mad Uncle Jack's Ex-Privates Dabble, No-Sir, Babcock and Glee cross out the word '*Mabel*' on the programmes and replace it with '*My Boy*'.

The stage itself, however, was most impressive, in the beautiful setting of the lower lawn with the lake beyond.

As Mr Dickens had promised his nephew, Fabian, the audience was made up of family members, both immediate and distant, and friends, including those members of the Thackery family not in prison. What Eddie knew and most others did not was that there were plain-clothed policemen in both the audience and 'mingling' backstage. They were plain clothed in that they were uniformed policemen out of uniform, not from a special division, and Eddie's fear had been that they might have stuck out like sore thumbs. He was impressed, however, by how well they blended in with the other misfits around them.

Mad Uncle Jack and Even Madder Aunt Maud sat in the front row. Dawkins sat next to EMAM with Annabelle on his lap. He just knew that she was going to bite him. It was only a matter of *when*. Even Madder Aunt Maud looked incomplete. It's the only way to describe it; rather like encountering someone you've only ever known with a beard after they've shaved it off. She was without Malcolm. She was Malcolmless. She hadn't seen him since Friday, when she'd been out walking with MUJ before Peevance had started firing those cabbages. She felt heartbroken. Guilty. Forlorn. How could she have put a baby crocodile – anyone or anything – above her beloved Malcolm? Now she was paying the price. She picked up her programme (which had somehow remained uncorrected). '*That's Mabel*: Being The Dramatic Early Years Of My Only Son Edmund,' she read. 'Excellent title!'

'Ridiculous!' snorted Mad Uncle Jack.

Backstage, Eddie was jiggling from one foot to

the other. Mr Pumblesnook gave him such a hearty slap on the back that Eddie could have sworn his teeth rattled.

'Nervous, me boy?' he asked,

'Very,' said Eddie. What he didn't say was that, quite apart from the play, he was nervous about what Dr Moot and others had in store, and what the detective chief inspector had in store for *them*.

'Stagefright is what fuels some of the great actors of our generation,' Mr Pumblesnook tried to reassure him. 'Frockle swears that his performances would be a mere shadow of what they are without the benefit of stagefright.'

Eddie wondered whether the actor-manager had made up Frockle on the spot. Frockle certainly sounded like a made-up name.

'Five minutes to curtain, Mr Pumblesnook,' said a boy a year or two younger than Eddie. A former inmate of St Horrid's, he'd only just been promoted to assistant stage manager since the boy who'd been *supposed* to be doing the job had disappeared.

'Thank you, Fishy!' said Mr Pumblesnook, the boy's name being Turbot. 'Nothing beats the excitement of a first night,' he said with the same enthusiasm that he'd said that nothing beat the excitement of the first read-through of a new play, or the first dress rehearsal, or a hundred-and-one

170

other things theatrical.

'Don't forget the announcement,' said Eddie.

'Your father's speech? How could I?'

'I mean the announcement of the reward for anyone who finds Malcolm. Mad Aunt Maud insisted that it be done before the curtain goes up, and by you. She's a great admirer of your performing skills, as you know.'

'She first saw me as Pompom in *All About Alex* if memory serves,' said the actor-manager, warming to EMAM once again now that rehearsals were over. 'She came up to me afterwards and presented me with a pair of opera glasses she'd stolen from the seat in front of her. Most generous.' He meant it.

'Positions, please!' said Fishy Turbot. The curtain was ready to rise.

Mr Pumblesnook walked onto the stage amid cheers from those he'd ordered to cheer, and ripples of polite applause from the others.

His speech was incredibly long and remarkably boring so let me give you the edited highlights, which are quite enough, I promise you.

'Ladies and gentlemen. Firstly, let me welcome you to the beautiful grounds of Awful End, as the guest of . . . *blah, blah, blah* . . . Secondly, let me introduce myself . . . *blah, blah, blah* . . . Tonight is a very special night. It's special, because the play you are about to see was written by Mr Laudanum Dickens about his own son, Edmund. And, if that weren't enough, not only will Edmund be playing the part of himself, but also, other members of the cast shall also be reliving events in which they too participated . . . *blah, blah, blah.* . . . and so to one correction, and one announcement. The first concerns the title of the play as it is printed upon the programmes you have before you . . . *blah, blah, blah* . . . The second concerns a missing stuffed stoat –'

'My Malcolm!' shouted EMAM, leaping to her feet. 'There's a substantial reward –'

'– and no questions will be asked of the one returning it,' said Mr Pumblesnook, attempting to seize back control of the moment.

'*Him,*' said EMAM.

'Him,' said the actor-manager, finally winding up his speech, with an all-that-it-remains-for-me-to-do section that lasted another eight-and-a-half minutes. Then it was curtains up.

Bunyon and Gherkin may not have known about the theft of A. C. Pryden's portrait of MUJ, but they certainly knew plenty about Harry 'Thunk' Scarple, Harry 'The Fingers' Morton and Doctor Samuel 'Moo-Cow' Moot.

'Scarple's called Thunk for two reasons,' Bunyon had told Eddie in the back of the carriage. 'First off, he got the nickname from falling down chimneys so often. It's the sound he makes when he hits the hearth. Secondly, as far as Harry Morton is concerned, he wants to be the only Harry in their little gang, and what he says goes.'

'What about the doctor?' Eddie had asked.

'No criminal record. We thought at first that Scarple and Morton might have been blackmailing him, then Gherkin discovered that it was revenge.'

'He's going to help them strip Awful End of all its finery,' the dwarf had explained.

'But revenge for what?' Eddie had said. 'He was the one who shot Mad Uncle Jack twice –'

'But on the one occasion,' Bunyon and Gherkin had said, together.

'Don't forget that your great-uncle won the ultimate prize, though, Master Edmund.'

'Even Madder Aunt Maud?'

'Even Madder Aunt Maud.'

Eddie found it hard to imagine his great-aunt as a prize. 'But, surely, if Dr Moot is as in love with Mad Aunt Maud as he claims to be, he wouldn't want to upset her by robbing her home?'

'Years of jealousy can do terrible things to a person,' said Gherkin. 'Dr Moot stopped seeing things straight long before your Aunt Hester hit him over the head with the end of the steakbeater. He has grown so jealous of Mad Major Dickens that it was easy for Thunk and Morton to get him to be their "inside man" on the job.'

Eddie had frowned at this. 'But if my Uncle Alfie hadn't been so ill, we'd never have called Dr Moot to Awful End.'

'It didn't matter. If Moot hadn't had the good fortune of being asked to attend your poor uncle, he'd have simply turned up on your front doorstep one day. He would have claimed it was a courtesy call: an old acquaintance taking over the medical practice and that. Once he had his foot in the door, he'd be able to return.'

The carriage had pulled up beside what turned out to be the other end of the alley that Eddie had followed Gherkin down. The three of them had stepped out, and Eddie had followed them through the door (almost) marked 'PRIVATE PROPERTY' (which was opened from the inside after Bunyon knocked on it with a series of *rat-a-tat-tats*). He found himself in the back of the police station.

'Saves me being seen walking through the front entrance,' Gherkin had explained. 'I don't want everyone knowing my business now, do I?'

This had led Eddie to ask the question he'd been dying to ask: why Gherkin had thrown the makeshift smoke bomb through the window. He'd guessed that it was to get them out of the house, but *why* exactly?

'We've had our eye on those three for a while,' the detective inspector – sorry, the detective *chief* inspector – had said, leading them into his office. 'It soon became obvious that their latest target was your home, but we want to catch them red-handed, so they can't deny it –'

'Which is why we did nothing to stop them getting that poor deranged Mr Peevance out of debtors' prison,' Gherkin had added.

'Precisely. But then Larkin disappeared.'

'Larkin?'

'Larkin. Larry Larkin. A member of Mr Pumblesnook's group of wandering theatricals.'

'Oh, I know who you mean,' Eddie had nodded. 'He's – he *was* – the assistant stage manager. I remember Mrs Pumblesnook saying that he'd gone missing. She didn't seem too concerned. She said he'd wandered off for a few days once before.'

'That's as maybe,' Gherkin had said.

'Maybe,' Bunyon had added, 'but we wanted to make sure that the boy hadn't overheard something he shouldn't, and been kidnapped by the gang. Morton, Scarple and Moot aren't murderers, but they may not be averse to locking some poor child up in a back room, so we had to be sure.' The detective chief inspector had personal experience of being locked in a trunk (against his will, obviously).

'But you couldn't send a bunch of peelers bursting in on them, because they'd know the game is up . . . so you did the smoke trick?'

'And in I went, only to find absolutely nothing. Which means they're either holding Larkin elsewhere, or he really has just wandered off for a few days.'

This had been a lot of information for Eddie to take in, but it all seemed to make a certain kind of sense. 'But won't the smoke trick make them suspicious that *something*'s going on?' he'd asked, just as the detective inspector had gone to sit on a large pile of books, which began to topple. The policeman grabbed the nearest thing, which was a bust of Queen Victoria, and both he and Her Majesty would have hit the floorboards if the acrobatic dwarf hadn't sprung to their rescue.

'A point well made, Master Edmund,' Bunyon had continued, completely unruffled as though

176

nothing had happened. 'Which is why we had the foresight to attach a note to the plumber's mate.'

The next obvious question was: 'What did it say?', so Eddie had asked it.

'MOOT GO HOME. WE DON'T WANT YOUR KIND HERE,' Gherkin had replied, with a mischievous grin.

'What kind is he?'

'That's the beauty of it, young Edmund. He can be any kind you like. It could be someone who doesn't like doctors, or droopy moustaches, or the way he pronounces his 'r's . . . He'll be racking his brains trying to work out who's got it in for him and why.'

'That's very clever,' Eddie had said.

'Ingenious,' Gherkin had agreed. 'It was the detective chief inspector's idea.'

See, dear readers? I told you he was a good policeman.

'We've also been surprisingly successful at eavesdropping on some of their conversations,' Bunyon had added. He'd straightened up the pile of books – gazetteers – and was gently lowering himself into a sitting position. 'And we know that they plan to steal whatever they plan to steal – in addition to the painting you tell us that they have already stolen – tomorrow evening during the first performance of *That's Mabel.*'

177

'*That's My Boy*,' Eddie had corrected him.

'That's not what it says on the posters and programmes,' Gherkin had told him.

Oh dear, Eddie had thought. Oh dear.

★

And now the curtain was up and the play had begun. Eddie was still wondering what 'valuables' the gang of three were after. It wasn't as though Awful End was one of those country houses stuffed with treasures and family heirlooms. MUJ and EMAM had rather a different approach to things. They liked what they liked and valued what they valued, regardless of its so-called value in the wider world. When Even Madder Aunt Maud was to die, many, many, many years after the events in this book, she was buried with her most treasured possession; a tatty old stuffed stoat. One of Mad Uncle Jack's most prized objects was a prune stone: the first thing his beloved Maud ever spat at him. If you're a sentimental old thing like me, you might be moved to tears by such things and mutter 'a price beyond rubies' into the nearest beard. If you're a thief, however, you might be annoyed and demand, 'Where's the good stuff?'

Mad Uncle Jack did have a safe – made by Dullard & Fisk of Birmingham in 1863 (according to the big metal badge-like thingumy on the front of it) – but he'd long since forgotten what was in it and lost the key. But there were also some valuable – in the money-money-money sense – pieces of silver and oil paintings to be had. And to have them, Harry Morton intended.

Episode 16
The Grand Finale

*In which the final curtain falls on
Eddie's further adventures*

Now, the more eagle-eyed amongst you might
just have spotted that the illustration above is
not a David Roberts original. In truth, some of you
might not consider it an illustration at all. I
confess: I drew it myself. Why? I'll tell you why,
because David is a very busy man – he must have a
cleaning job on the side, or something – so he
agreed to do a certain number of pictures for this
book, and no more. Then, because there was *so*
much to fit into this final adventure, I had to make
the book a little longer than I thought I would . . .
and there aren't enough pictures to go round. But
will I let a small thing such as that defeat me? No
way. Let the story continue.

Whilst all eyes were (apparently) on the stage, the lovely Daniella's father and Harry Morton were studying the safe in what had once been MUJ's study. Dr Moot had told them exactly where he'd found it and they went straight there. They weren't even going to attempt to open the safe in the study. The plan was to take it elsewhere and then to blow the door off with dynamite. The whole point of a safe was that it was designed to be difficult to move. This particular one wasn't bolted to the floor or set in concrete, but it was incredibly heavy. The two Harrys had come armed with some special kind of hoist (or lifting device) and a very tough-looking metal trolley to wheel it away on.

Whilst Eddie was performing on the stage in the grounds in an early scene (where he learns that his parents have gone yellow, crinkly around the edges and smell of old hot-water bottles), Scarple and Morton managed to ease the safe onto the trolley. It was hard work, and they'd worked up a good sweat.

'Now what?' asked Scarple.

'We sticks to the plan, that's what, Thunk.'

'Remind me.'

'The solid silver stuff in the back of them cupboards Moo-Cow told us about.' Morton unfolded a rough plan of some of the rooms that Dr Moot had sketched out for them. 'Our very own treasure map,' he grinned.

181

They hurried from room to room, putting their booty into the large sack that they'd initially used to carry the hoist into the house.

'Beats workin' for a livin',' said the chimney-sweep with a smile. Next, they started taking the oil paintings off the walls.

Now came the tricky part. With everyone outside and them inside, knowing exactly where the 'good stuff' was, they could work quickly and efficiently, but now they had to get the stuff out of the house and off the grounds.

Fortunately for this pair of thieves, there was an ancient path crossing the Dickens estate, which anyone and everyone had a right to walk along (or ride a horse along, though not a mule or a donkey, apparently) without permission. At one point, it passed surprisingly close to the house itself, and – to give the Dickenses some privacy – hedges had been planted either side of it for this stretch. What's more, it was on the opposite side of the house to the stage.

Part of the plan was simply to tie off the end of the silver-filled sack and to toss it over the hedge onto the Way (as the path was called locally). The path was rarely used and they could simply collect their booty later.

Wheeling the trolley off the grounds with the safe and a pile of pictures on top would be a little harder. Morton unfolded the sheet he'd brought with him especially for the occasion and threw it over the trolley. On it was printed:

PUMBLESNOOK'S

If stopped or challenged, they'd claim to be a part of the night's proceedings, moving props and scenery for *That's My Boy*.

Harry Morton admired his own handiwork, straightening the sheet at one corner. 'A very professional job though I says so meself, Thu–'

There was a crash from the next room, as though someone had kicked a vase or something. Scarple dashed over to the door, as nimbly and as silently as his limp allowed. There was no point in hiding and hoping that whoever it might be would go away. They'd left the sack in there, and they weren't about to give it up without a fight.

Scarple looked left and right; under the table and behind the door; and even in a cupboard or two. No one. He tied off the top of the sack, and headed for the back door. 'I'll just toss this onto the Way, an' be right back,' he told Morton. The sack was good and heavy, and Daniella's father was thinking of all the lovely things this silver would buy.

It was some twenty-five minutes later, when the two thieves were pushing the heavily-laden trolley across a stretch of grass, that Even Madder Aunt Maud went and spoiled everything. The play had reached the stage where Malcolm appeared, and the sight of a pretend Malcolm made her pine for the real one even more keenly. She'd got up from her seat and gone for a walk.

Morton – who was, most definitely, the brains of the outfit – hadn't taken into consideration the effect the weight of the safe on the trolley might have when moving it. The plan had been to wheel it boldly down the gravel drive, but you try wheeling something that heavy down gravel. It sank like a stubborn elephant digging its heels in (if elephants have heels). They were lucky that they even managed to get it off the drive and back into the house. This change of plan meant that they'd have to push it across grass, including a small stretch that would be in full view of anyone in the audience who chose to glance to their left . . .

. . . and now here was Mad Aunt Maud.

'Beautiful evenin', ma'am,' said Morton, raising his cap.

'Drop dead,' she said.

'I beg your pardon?' said Morton, with righteous indignation.

'Not you, nincompoop,' she muttered. 'I was talking to myself.'

The two Harrys dared not stop pushing the

trolley, for fear of it sinking into the lawn and becoming lodged. The upper lawn was on a slight slope, sweeping down to the lower lawn and the ornamental lake. Their rather one-sided conversation with EMAM caused a momentary lapse in concentration. Morton let go of the trolley just as it started to roll down the slope, Scarple running to keep up with it, his hands still on the handle. Morton reached out and grabbed it too, but the laws of physics dictate that something feels a lot heavier if it's rolling down hill gathering speed. (But don't put that in an answer to an exam question, just in case I'm wrong.) Soon both men were forced to let go of the trolley as it gathered nuts in May.* They chased after it and so did Eddie's great-aunt.

'This is fun!' she screeched.

It was her shout which made a member of the audience look up and see a large trolley hurtling towards the rows of people watching the first-night performance. The man in question, Johnny Bluff, had been a big game hunter. He'd loved endangering species in Africa and India, until one day his rifle jammed and he was charged by a very angry bull elephant indeed. He'd escaped with his life, and a few squashed toes, but had become a

* I'm sorry, that should, of course, read momentum.

185

bag of nerves . . . and now something else was charging his way.

'Elephant attack!' he shouted, leaping to his feet.

Even Mr Pumblesnook would have been hard-pressed keeping all eyes on the stage with that interruption. In fact, this was one of the rare moments when the actor-manager was in the wings.

The audience jumped up and scattered, knocking chairs hither and thither (which is not dissimilar to here, there and everywhere).

Logically, this would have been the moment for Harry 'The Fingers' Morton and Harry 'Thunk' Scarple to turn and run. They must have known in their heart of hearts that the safe and its contents were never going to be theirs after all. But human nature's not like that. You let go of something and it runs away, and you chase after it, so on they went, through the small crowd and beyond.

The own-clothed policemen dropped all pretence of being friends, relatives or theatre-lovers and gave chase, but – jumping from the edge of the stage – Eddie had a head start . . . which is how he came to be only seconds behind Morton when the thief tripped over something, and fell.

The something in question was the tail of some kind of stuffed stoat, which had been buried in the mud, nose-first, by a young crocodile, perhaps intent on removing a rival to her mistress's affections. (Who knows what goes on in the mind of a young female crocodile? Not I.)

'Malcolm!' screeched Even Madder Aunt Maud, redder-faced from all that running than any beetroot's face could ever be. She pulled him out of the ground like a gardener plucks out a carrot, and there followed a reunion to rival any scene – romantic or sentimental – in any film/movie/flick/ motion picture ever made.

Eddie's father, meanwhile, had nabbed Morton before he'd fully struggled to his feet. The rage at his play being interrupted was so great that it seemed to give him super-human strength. If someone had been in a position to hand him a baby-grand piano there and then, he felt that he could have ripped it in two. With his teeth. Holding on to a snarling villain was a piece of cake/a stroll in the park/a walk in the rain.

Which left the chimney sweep Scarple who, true to his nickname Thunk, was the victim of yet another little accident. The trolley must also have hit Malcolm and the safe had lurched off it, landing on him with a loud 'thunk!', of all things. The force of the jolt had also made the door fly open. I'll write that again, just to make sure you got it: *made the door fly open*. The safe had been unlocked all the time. Its contents were now littered across the grass.

A puzzled Eddie picked up a square black object, the size of a floor tile. It *was* a black floor tile, and the safe had been full of them. Now where in heavens could they have come from? Your guess is as good as mine. As to why Mad Uncle Jack had put them in the safe in the first place, I doubt even he knew. Anyone who's journeyed through all six Eddie Dickens books with me will know that M-a-d at the start of his name is there for a reason.

'You're both under arrest,' said Detective Chief Inspector Bunyon, arriving on the scene at last, a little out of breath.

'What for?' sneered Morton. 'Wheelin' a bunch of floor tiles around a garden? What will we get for that, then? A slap on the wrist?'

'What about this, then?' said Bunyon, stepping aside to let two officers bring forward a large sack between them. 'Once you threw that sack over the hedge into the Way, you'd taken it off Major Dickens's property without permission. There's a word for that: theft.'

'Prove it was us what threw it,' said Morton.

'Yeah,' said Scarple trying to sound defiant, but they could tell that he had no fight in him.

Bunyon opened the sack, then, looking into it, opened his eyes wide with surprise. The sack started to *move*.

'You!' gasped Scarple, as Gherkin stepped out of the sack and into the evening air, as though it was the most natural thing in the world.

The dwarf was nursing a nasty bump on his head. 'Not the best place to hide under the circumstances, I'll admit,' he said. 'But the one place you didn't look . . . *and* I was able to hear everything you two villains said, whilst, at the same time, keeping the stolen silver in sight.'

Detective Chief Inspector Bunyon gave the two Harrys the benefit of one of his withering stares. 'So now all you have to do is tell us what you did with the painting, and –'

'They don't have the painting,' said Eddie.

'Wh–?' said Gherkin.

'–at?' said Bunyon.

Eddie walked over to A. C. Pryden who was standing amongst the semicircle of onlookers who had gathered round. 'I only realised it this afternoon, Mr Pryden, but there was something wrong with your story about leaving the picture while you went to get some more writing paper downstairs. You wanted the picture to *appear* to have been stolen, without any of us in the household being under suspicion. That's why you seized the opportunity to say it had been stolen at a time when we all had alibis, as we gathered together on the lawn. That's why you didn't want

190

the police involved. That's why you were reluctant to speak to Mr Peevance in his police cell. You knew he had nothing to do with it.'

'Is this true, sir?' demanded Bunyon, whose men had now freed Scarple from beneath the safe and were putting him in handcuffs.

'Yes,' said the painter, sounding like the most guilty penguin anyone of us is ever likely to meet.

'But why? That's what I don't understand,' said Eddie.

By way of an answer, A. C. Pryden stuck his hand in a pocket and pulled out a crumpled letter. He handed it to the detective chief inspector.

'Can't read,' he said, handing it to the desk sergeant, who thought that it was jolly unfair of him to have been called away from his desk. (And he didn't like not wearing his uniform with the lovely shiny buttons either.) 'Won't read,' he said, passing it to Eddie. So Eddie read it. Aloud.

'*Dear Mr Pryden, I regret to inform you that, due to a simple clerical error, you have been commissioned to paint a portrait of the wrong Major Dickens.*' Eddie gulped. '*Whilst it was the War Office's intention that you paint Major* Jock *Dickens, a fine soldier who has distinguished himself in a series of campaigns during an illustrious career spanning many decades –*' Eddie paused at this point. He wasn't sure that he wanted to read any more out loud.

'A typing error meant that you ended up painting my uncle instead?' said his father.

'That's the gist of it,' the portrait painter nodded. 'And I felt it would be shabby and disrespectful to simply pack up and leave, but neither did I want a public unveiling. If I could convince you in the family that the painting had gone, then those at the War Office could inform the Major themselves, at a more appropriate time and in a more respectful manner.'

'Very noble sentiments indeed, but you could have wasted valuable police time,' said Bunyon. 'However, seeing as how things have worked out . . .'

'Thank you,' said Pryden.

When Malcolm had been washed, Harry 'The Fingers' Morton and Harry 'Thunk' Scarple taken off to the police station (and Moot arrested in Harborough Wensley, trying to pretend that he was someone else, simply by having shaved off his moustache), Fabian asked Eddie the all-important question: 'What was it that Mr Pryden said that made you realise that he'd made up the whole thing about the painting having been stolen?'

And here's the sad part. I've no idea what Eddie's reply was.

A shame that. There's no record of his explanation anywhere that I could find.

Still, this isn't a detective novel with all the

192

suspects gathered in the library for the grand unmasking. This is an Eddie Dickens adventure. We're here for . . . for . . . What are we here for? Now, that would be a profound question to end on.

*

But I can't leave it there, of course. There are plenty of other questions I *can* answer. I can, for example tell you that, though the first night's performance of *That's Mabel* was abandoned, despite Mr and Mrs Pumblesnook's chorus of 'The show must go on!', it was performed two nights later (on the Wednesday). It was, by all accounts, appalling. The writing was patchy to say the least, and Mr Pumblesnook performing so many of the meaty roles led to terrible confusion as to who he was supposed to be when, especially during the scenes where he was playing three or more characters on stage at the same time. Eddie managed to remember all of his lines and put in a creditable performance.

Mad Uncle Jack said to him afterwards, 'You made a very believable Edmund Dickens, young man. Please call upon me one day at your convenience.' He handed Eddie a dried sea horse.

The missing boy, Larkin, turned up a few days after the abandoned first night performance, smelling of mothballs. He'd somehow managed to lock himself in an old laundry cupboard in one of the many disused parts of the house.

A week or so later, Gherkin left to work with an Inspector Ryman up north. His working for the police in 'an undercover capacity' meant that, once people knew what he was up to, he had to move elsewhere. The reason why Fabian had thought he'd recognised him that first morning was because their paths had, indeed, crossed fleetingly before. Gherkin had been working for a Sergeant Kelpitt in a part of Hampshire when Fabian's gypsy family had been passing through.

Lance Peevance had, indeed, been unaware of his role in the plan; to cause a distraction whilst Moo-Cow Moot had one last good look around before his accomplices paid a visit. When he was eventually released from prison, he moved to the distant village of Lower Upton (or Upper Lowton) where he led a quiet life, building a little chapel with his own hands, over an eleven-year period. This greatly impressed the other inhabitants, until the building fell down one blustery November morning, injuring the village mascot (a goose called Tawny).

Once Fabian's father stopped eating any more lucky heather, let the rest pass through his system, and (finally) took his medication (in liquid rather than tablet form), he made a splendid recovery. The original cough was cured with some syrup or other. Discovering that Dr Moot had been a no-good scoundrel, Aunt Hetty soon got over the guilt at having nearly brained him.

As for the older Dickenses, they went on doing what the older Dickenses did best. And Eddie? For him, the best was yet to come.

THE END
of the Further Adventures

A NOTE FROM THE AUTHOR

You've been a wonderful audience.
Thank you and goodnight.

The Philip Ardagh Club

COLLECT some fantastic **Philip Ardagh** merchandise.

WHAT YOU HAVE TO DO:

You'll find numbered tokens to collect in all Philip Ardagh's fiction books published after 01/04/05. There are 2 tokens in each hardback and 1 token in each paperback. Cut them out and send them to us complete with the form below (or a photocopy of the form) and you'll get these great gifts:

> **2 tokens** = a Philip Ardagh poster
> **3 tokens** = a Philip Ardagh mousemat
> **4 tokens** = a Philip Ardagh pencil case and stationery set

Please send the form, together with your tokens or photocopies of them, to:

Philip Ardagh promotion, Faber and Faber Ltd, 3 Queen Square, London, WC1N 3AU.

Please ensure that each token has a different number.

1. This offer can not be used in conjunction with any other offer and is non transferable. 2. No cash alternative is offered. 3. If under 18 please get permission and help from a parent or guardian to enter. 4. Please allow at least 28 days delivery. 5. No responsibility can be taken for items lost in the post. 6. This offer will close on 31/04/07. 7. Offer open to readers in the UK and Ireland ONLY.

Name: ....

Address: ....

....

....

Town: ....

Postcode: ....

Age & Date of Birth: ....

Girl or boy: ....

Philip Ardagh Club
token number 10

Philip Ardagh Club
token number 11

For more infomation and competitions join the Philip Ardagh Club on-line.
Visit www.philipardagh.com